MW01088669

"The author has a unique style of writing. She has her story development under control, no matter the twist that she adds at any point… I'd rate it **four out of four stars.**"

— -ONLINE BOOK CLUB

Lee offers skillful plotting that unveils several surprises readers won't see coming, both in the thriller and romance departments."

— -KIRKUS REVIEW

"I could see the Nubble Lighthouse in the distance. When the characters walked through the sandy beaches falling in love or experiencing heartbreak, I, too, could hear the music wafting over from the nearby piano bar."

— -ALLISON NOWAK- REEDSY

"I was so engrossed in this book that I forgot to eat. The suspense it contained is top-notch. I must commend the author for this masterpiece."

— - ELENDU EKECHUKWU- READER

NEVER IN A BILLION

A NOVEL

STACY LEE

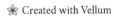 Created with Vellum

For my husband, Paul. You are my one in a billion.

ACKNOWLEDGMENTS

I would once again like to thank Lynn and her team at Red Adept Editing. I couldn't do this without you! Also, another huge thank-you to Julie and her team at Spark Creative for designing yet another gorgeous cover. I am beyond blessed to work with all of you.

Thank you to Kris and the team at the Talking Book. Collaborating with you and your team on the audiobooks for *The Hundredth Time Around* and *Future Plans* has been an incredible experience. I can't wait to bring the characters from *Never in a Billion* to life with you!

Also, a huge thank-you to Allen Redwing and the team at Bookscribs. Working with you to develop the screenplay for *The Hundredth Time Around* has been a dream come true. Your dedication to the project and your creative insight have been nothing short of fantastic. Allen, I can't thank you enough for meeting with me week after week. I can't wait until movie night!

I would also like to thank the local gift shops in the York and Ogunquit, Maine, communities. Whispering Sands, Beach Funatic, the Nubble Lighthouse Giftshop, and the Ogunquit Drug Store, I can't thank you enough!

Thank you to my husband, Paul Barbagallo. I could never do this without you. You continue to encourage, support, and inspire me every day. Thank you for believing in me the way that you do and for being my rock. I love you with all my heart, and I thank God each day for you. Thank you for being such an amazing husband and supportive father... You truly are *my* one in a billion.

Thank you to my mother-in-law, Shirley Barbagallo. We know you are shining down from Heaven, but we so wish you were here. Thank you for bringing me to York Beach and for making us paint pictures of the lighthouse. Our lives have been forever changed.

Also, a huge thank-you to my children, Paul and Lucy—to think you are both in middle school this year! Paul, I love watching you grow in confidence, especially on the football field, and Lucy... nobody shines brighter than you on that stage! Keep dreaming, guys—I can't wait to watch you both live your dreams. Paul in the NFL, and Lucy on Broadway. You are what you believe!

Thank you to my family, my biggest cheerleaders! My parents, Karen and Dan DeBruyckere; sister, Kate Giglio, and her husband Joe; my sister-in-law, Cheri Grassi, and her husband Mike; my aunt, Patricia Fishwick; and my brother, Dan DeBruyckere Jr. Writers can only write what we know, and I have all of you to thank for showing me how to love.

Thank you to my friends, my biggest supporters! Thank you, Stacie Swanson, for your continued encouragement. I appreciate your friendship and can't wait until our Disney vacation in 2022! Thank you, Marisa and Josh Berlin, for your encouragement and for your friendship. Marisa, we are going to make the best old ladies.

A huge thank-you to my best friend, Kara Holloway. Thank you for standing by me and for supporting me and reminding me each day that you are proud of me. I love doing life with you, Court, and the kids! You truly are the best friend I could ever ask for.

A special thank-you to Jaclyn Hannan and Aaron Pawelek. I wouldn't be where I am today without your constant guidance, encouragement, and support. Thank you for keeping me grounded and reminding me of the important things in life.

Thank you, Rob Hulse, for everything you have done for me. Not only am I physically stronger and healthier since we started working together; I am mentally and emotionally the strongest I have ever been. Your positive attitude and your energy are contagious. Thank you for boosting my confidence and for kicking my butt into shape.

Thank you to the community of York Beach, Maine, and the Cape Neddick community. You have been so receptive to the Nubble Light Series, and I can't thank you enough for your support. Thank you to Marie and all my friends at Fox's Lobster House in Cape Neddick. Your support means more than you know.

Of course, I need to thank you, the reader! Thank you for reading my novels and for all of your feedback. It brings such joy to my heart that you are falling in love with the characters just as I have. May you continue to love without hesitation and dream the biggest dreams... Remember, nothing is impossible. There is always a way. I hope you enjoy book three of the Nubble Light Series. Thank you, and God bless!

A NOTE TO THE READER

This is the third book in the Nubble Light Series. The first book, *The Hundredth Time Around*, was published in January of 2021. *Future Plans* is the second book in the series and was released in April of 2021. *Never in a Billion* is the third book, and book four is already in the works! Although each book in the Nubble Light Series can stand alone, I highly encourage you to read them in order, beginning with *The Hundredth Time Around*.

The Nubble Light Series was inspired by my visit to York Beach in 2020. My mother-in-law, Shirley Barbagallo, brought me and my family to visit during what ended up being some of the last months of her life. During this visit, we fell in love with the beaches of York, Maine, Cape Neddick, and the Nubble Lighthouse. Because of this, the Nubble Lighthouse holds a special place in my heart.

Also, please be on the lookout for a special miniseries I am writing for elementary-aged children from the point of view of dogs at daycare. Please email stacybarbagallo@gmail.com or check out Facebook for more information.

PART ONE

PROLOGUE

ONE WEEK BEFORE THE BIG DAY

efinition of never/not in a thousand/million/billion years—
*used as a strong way of saying that something is **extremely** **unlikely or impossible**. —Merriam Webster*

IMPOSSIBLE. *Such a crummy word. The mere principle of identifying something as extremely unlikely, or not going to happen, disturbs me in ways that are unexplainable. I often come across as overly optimistic, naïve, or even childish at times, simply because I truly believe that nothing is unattainable or unsolvable; there is simply always a way.*

Consider the New England Patriots in Superbowl XLIX. My party guests vanished back to the comfort of their own sofas long before the end of the game. Although I insisted that two minutes was plenty of time to pull around, they disagreed, leaving me to witness the greatest comeback of all time unfold before my very eyes—victory.

A simple Google search will reveal concepts throughout history that were once considered impossible. Automobiles, lightbulbs, air travel, television, and computers for starters. I sometimes chuckle to myself when I think of the satisfaction that must have amounted when award-winning inventors or well-educated scientists stared down their critics with glee and gloated, "Told you so." And what about those that allowed their dreams and greatest desires to be oppressed by others? Imagine the billions of ideas, successes, and relationships that could have been?

So, if that's the case and impossible things can be possible, then why is it that we get so irrationally stuck and paralyzed with fear when we consider what we desire to be unlikely, impossible, or in simpler terms... not going to happen? I, for one, will jiggle that Magic 8-Ball until as I see it, YES, appears in the blue triangle, securing my destiny in my own hands.

What I hope you can take from today's article, dear reader, is never give up hope. Just because the thing (or person, for that matter) you desire seems remarkably out of reach doesn't mean it can't happen. The only thing worse than giving up hope on something you want more than anything... is regret.

"Never in a million years will that happen," you say... never in a billion? Well, my friends, you just might be that one in a billion. Never give up hope.

UNTIL NEXT TIME,
Miss Taken
Xoxoxoxoxo

CHAPTER ONE- NOW

MAGGIE

ONE MONTH BEFORE THE BIG DAY

The familiar click-clack of my black Jimmy Choos against the newly paved parking lot provides an unexpected sense of comfort as the last drop of my morning coffee trickles down. I nod and smile at the familiar faces of my coworkers and stop only to toss my coffee cup in the nearest waste basket. I am already running twenty minutes late this morning, and an overwhelming sense of panic ripples through me. *Today is the day,* I think.

I reach for the metal handle of the front door to Wells Valley Cove and Retirement Center, but it swings open before I even make contact.

"Morning, Miss Thatcher," Seth greets me.

I roll my eyes and adjust my burgundy Kate Spade tote bag with one hand and fix the collar of my black suit coat with the other. "Seth," I snarl, determined to avoid eye contact. "We dated for like three years. I've told you before— you don't need to call me Miss Thatcher."

"Just doing my job, *Miss* Thatcher."

I cave and unglue my gaze from the floor and make eye contact with him. He smirks at me, and it doesn't take long

3

before my insides tingle, and I am immediately sucked into another universe through his irresistible baby blues. *Of course, my ex-boyfriend must be Zac Efron's doppelgänger.* I pause and make a mental note to keep my next relationship out of the workplace. "Have a nice day, Seth," I state politely, just as I have practiced every day for the past three weeks and two days since our breakup.

I squeeze by him, allowing the sides of our bodies to touch, and collect my ash-blond hair awkwardly over one shoulder.

"You look nice today, Maggie."

I stop short and turn toward him; the warmth of his breath against my cheek weakens my knees. I pause, face him again, and wonder if he means it or if he is simply kissing my ass. "Thank you."

He sticks his hands in his pockets and looks me up and down. "Interview day?"

I feel blood rush to my face and pray that he can't see the effect he has on me. "It is," I say, rummaging through my bag and retrieving my favorite berry lipstick. I pop it open and begin reapplying, a nervous habit of mine.

"Maggie, I—" he starts but stops because a family is entering the building and he needs to open the door. I use this opportunity to deposit my lipstick back in my bag and scurry away.

"Welcome to Wells Valley Cove and Retirement Center," he says, his voice fading slowly from a distance.

I retrieve my phone from my pocket and sneak a peek at the time; there are two hours until my big interview.

"Maggie!" he shouts. I stop in my tracks and spin around once more.

I raise my eyebrows, clearly annoyed, and mouth the word *What?*

"Happy birthday!" he hollers.

4

I shake my head and sigh, annoyed because Seth knows how much I *hate* my birthday. "Thanks, Seth, really."

"Twenty-eight has never looked so good!"

I cringe and pick up the pace as I hustle down the carpeted hallway toward my office, trying my best to disregard the happy-birthday wishes from those around me thanks to Seth Jenson and his pathetic attempt to win me back. I grasp the brass doorknob and pause for a beat. My lips form into a soft smile, and for some reason, I can't remember why we broke up in the first place.

* * *

My FINGERS TAP briskly against my laptop keys as I finish my last email response of the morning. The clock on the upper-right part of my screen is taunting me. My interview is in exactly one hour. I sigh and reach my hands up overhead in a long and extended stretch. I inhale, exhale, and reassure myself that this will be a piece of cake. Although I love my job as director of activities and wellness, it has been my dream to be promoted to an administrator position. My experiences and my time at WVC ensured that I would be a perfect fit for such a position, but until now, I didn't have the necessary degree to back that up. However, my newly completed master's degree in the field is sure to seal the deal; the opening as nursing home management and administrator is sure to be mine… I just need to make it through the interview in one piece.

I close my laptop and nervously spin from side to side in my office chair before rising from my seat and checking my skirt for wrinkles and evidence of dog hair in the mirror. I don't always wear suits to the office, but this is in fact interview day, and my father instilled in me the importance of dressing for success since my kindergarten graduation.

The buzzing of my cell from my mahogany desk startles me, interrupting my thoughts, and I smile when I see a text message from West on my screen. I lean against my desk and swipe open the text.

West: *Happy 28th to my best friend (insert inappropriate shirtless strippers in party hats)*

I smile and shake my head, realizing that he is the only person in the entire world who could wish me happy birthday and live to talk about it.

Maggie: *LOL. Thank you.*

West: *Any big birthday plans?*

Maggie: *Nope. Just here at work, hoping everyone forgets that it's my birthday.*

West: *Don't you have your interview today?*

Maggie: *Yup... soon actually (insert scared emoji)*

West: *You are going to crush it, Mags. You always do.*

I start to type back, but my screen is taken over by an incoming call. Kendra's name appears on my screen, and my heart crumbles. "Not today!" I plead with the universe. "Please, not today."

I shake my head from side to side and answer the phone on speaker, kicking off my shoes before I start to speak. I already know this is bad news because Kendra Ferguson only calls me during the day about lunch—or if Art Young has gotten into trouble again—and it isn't time for lunch.

"Please tell me this isn't what I think it is," I beg into my cell.

"Oh, I *wish* I were calling for your Chipotle order."

"What happened?"

"Art is down at the water, and he is refusing to come in. I can get someone else to handle it, Maggie, you have a big day today. It's just that you told me to always call you first... you know... when it comes to *Art*."

I dash over to the large picture window that overlooks

our private beach and pull back the turquoise curtains. The view from my office is truly breathtaking. The sunlight resonates against the dark surface of the ocean water under almost-cloudless blue sky. When I arrived this morning, it was low tide, the sand extending out for what seemed like miles. But now, the tide is coming in, leaving a significant amount of ocean and very little beach.

"I don't see him, Kendra," I groan. "What happened this time?"

Kendra sighs, sounding openly frustrated. "He just really wanted to go to the beach. I explained to him that our day is structured now that he is no longer in independent living… but he just barked at me like he was some kind of… I don't know… animal or something."

I shield my eyes from the sunlight with my palm and scope out the area, searching for Art Young, my eighty-two-year-old beach-going fugitive. "I still don't see him. Are you sure he went outside?"

"Yes, I am sure."

I switch my gaze from the shore and scan the ocean. Sure enough, Art Young, fully clothed in his khaki pants and Hawaiian shirt, is wading knee-deep in the Atlantic. "What the—"

"What is it?" Kendra asks.

I reach for my bottom desk drawer and grab the flip-flops that I keep for times such as these. "He's in the freaking water!" I squeal. I toss my suit jacket onto my chair and head out of my office, phone in hand.

"Oh, no, Maggie. Why don't you let me handle this? Or security, even? You have your interview."

My hand slides along the banister as my feet flip and flop down the concrete steps. "Because." I sigh. "It's Art Young we are talking about. You *know* how important he is to me."

* * *

I CHECK the time on my cell phone, realizing that I only have forty minutes until my interview. I need to act fast; I fling my cell down on a blue-and-white-striped beach chair and begin rolling up my blouse sleeves. I'm about twenty yards from Art, who is now waist-deep in the water, floating over the waves like a pesky seagull, grinning from ear to ear.

I kick off my flip-flops and call out to him as calmly as I can in this moment. "Nice day for a swim?"

If he hears me, he is choosing to ignore me. I clench my fists by my sides and count to ten before calling to him once more. "Art! You need to come back in! Swimming time isn't until *after* lunch."

I'm not concerned about Art's swimming ability. Not only was he a lifeguard during his prime years, but he was also quite the surfer. I tighten my jaw and shake my head in aggravation. Of course, he can hear me; he is simply choosing to pretend I don't exist. I look around again, searching for signs of WVC Security. If Art gets in trouble with security, he could lose outside time all together or even get kicked out of the facility. *Not on my watch,* I think to myself. I tug my skirt up to my knees and begin to kick through the chilly ocean water. He peeks at me with one eye open and grins again, almost like he has planned this little excursion. "I have my interview today, Art! Why don't you come in, and we can talk about it?"

With this, Art lies down on his back and continues floating. His khakis have become transparent, and I can see the outline of his tighty-whities. His Hawaiian shirt sticks to his skin like a wetsuit, and his thinning silver hair glistens against the early-afternoon sun.

I side-glance over my shoulder and spot a security guard heading our way. I hold up a finger as if to say, *One minute,* and turn back toward my friend, thankful for the positive rapport I have established with the WVC Security Team. But I know that I only have so long until they, too, will need to follow typical processes and procedures. "Art!" I snap, less patient this time. "You are going to get in trouble again," I warn like I am scolding a four-year-old child.

Art shoots his eyes open just as larger waves crash over him. "That's the problem, Maggie," he barks. "I should be able to come out here whenever I damn well please."

I nod my head in agreement, attempting with every piece of my soul to empathize with him. Art was one of the first residents at Wells Valley Cove. He came to live at the facility when he was in his early sixties. Back then, he started as an independent-living resident; basically, he was functioning on his own and could utilize whatever amenities at WVC and could come and go as he pleased. That was, until Art started to show signs that he couldn't take care of himself like he used to. He had fallen in the shower, and it had been almost twenty-four hours before anyone realized. Transitioning into assisted living and needing more care than before was a tough pill for him to swallow. I, too, would struggle with my freedom being ripped away. The idea of needing to ask permission before taking a swim was enough to soften my tough exterior and genuinely level with him. I mean, the guy hurt himself in the shower, not in the ocean. "I know. Why don't we go talk about it up on the beach?"

"Why don't we talk about it out *here?*"

I sigh and shimmy my skirt up as high as I can without exposing my rear end to the audience of retirement folk that has gathered on the beach around us—most of them being from the crew that Art was spending most of his time with prior to his transfer to assisted living.

I kick through the waves and shudder as chilly water splashes up around me, but I am no stranger to the sixty-degree waters of the Atlantic. I cringe anyway, envisioning myself sitting before the interview panel, looking like a drowned rat.

"Hi, Maggie," Art greets calmly.

I bite my lip and try to hide my aggravation. "What's going on, Art?"

"Interview today?" He is speaking to me, but his eyes remain closed as he floats over the waves, happy as a freaking clam.

A large wave heads our way, and I turn my back to it, allowing the frigid water to smack my backside and lift my skirt. "Ugh," I cry out. "I'm trying to help you, Art, but this is ridiculous."

Art sits up, chuckles, and collapses into an incoming wave. He emerges from the tide and shakes the water out of his silver tresses and frowns. "I should be able to swim *whenever* I want," he barks. He sinks into the water and swims back toward me, his long strokes those of an Olympic athlete, not of a man in his early eighties.

"Okay," I respond. "Like I said, we can talk about it on the beach. Maybe… maybe I can even talk to my father about it."

I hate to play the dad card, but there is no better time than the present. My father, Gary Thatcher, purchased WVC back in 1999. He is known throughout the Maine community for one thing and one thing only: investing in and remodeling one of the most successful retirement communities and nursing homes in New England. Not only did he purchase the land and the original facility, but because of the large sum of money my grandparents left him in their will, he was able to invest in the project on his own, creating a luxurious and affordable way for the southern Maine folk to retire together, by a place dear to their hearts—the ocean. The truth is, however, that he won't have much leverage when it comes to Art's privileges. I know this because it won't be the first time I bring up Art Young with my father.

Art hesitates for a moment and studies me carefully. "We go way back, you and me," he reminds me, his tone solemn and steady.

"Yes, we do."

"Don't you remember what I taught you? All those years ago?"

I examine him closely, and for a moment, I am not twenty-eight-year-old Maggie Thatcher anymore. I am a naïve and vulnerable seventeen-year-old girl, a troublemaker who got caught up with the wrong crowd. Standing before me is Art, my friend and mentor, and I realize that although this whole situation is silly, he isn't entirely wrong. Art should be able to go to the beach whenever he damn well pleases. Art needs the ocean like most people need air. "Yes," I state firmly. "I remember what you taught me."

"Then why, after all this time, do you need a new job? Why would you leave the activities department? Why would you leave *me*?"

My heart all but shatters into a million pieces as I realize that this isn't about Art and his recreational swimming restrictions; this is about *me*. Art is afraid of losing me. This isn't completely a surprise, as I understood that taking a position on the admin team would, in fact, mean less time with the residents. But I made a promise with myself to stay connected with them, even if I'm not directly involved with their daily living situations.

"You are a *people* person, Maggie. They are going to lock you up in a cubicle and put you on the Zoom all day. You know that, right?"

I chuckle at his comment as I wade through the icy water and take his hand in mine. "The Zoom doesn't scare me." I laugh. "Art, I'm not leaving WVC. I will still be working—"

Art holds his free hand up, stops me midsentence, and grins like a child up to no good. "Swim with me, Maggie," he pleads. "Swim with your old pal Art."

Something about the urgency in his voice causes me to plop down next to him without hesitation. My body temperature is finally regulating, but now the water is causing my new and very expensive skirt to float up over me like a parachute. But Art is right. As I lay my head back, allowing my hair to flow freely over each breaking wave, an unexpected sense of peace surrounds me. Art Young has a way of reminding me who I am and where I come from. If he needs me to swim with him, then, well… I am going to swim.

We lie there, Art and I, floating for what feels like hours but is probably just minutes, and I am reminded of some of the life lessons and principles he has taught me over the years; suddenly, my job interview is the farthest thing from my mind… which is good, because I don't have anything to wear.

"Hey!" A familiar voice jolts me back to reality, and my eyes snap open in surprise. "Nice day for a swim, or what?"

Standing over me is the tall and handsome figure of West Young. I shriek, unable to believe my own eyes, forgetting for a second that I am swimming in my interview clothes. I carefully remove my hand from Art's as he struggles to rise to his feet. My attempt to stand fails, and after two awkward steps backward, I am trapped in an incoming wave. My skirt puffs up around me once more as I flounder to regain my balance, wiping the water out of my eyes with my fingers. My vision is blurry, but when he comes into focus—his brunette hair, dark eyes, athletic build, boyish grin… I realize I'm *not* dreaming. West has come home.

"What are you doing with my grandfather?" he chuckles.

"West! West! Is it really you?" I shriek.

"Westly," Art stammers. "Westly, you're supposed to be in

Arizona."

West kicks through the waves, grabs my waist, and picks me up, allowing my toes to tickle the surface of the water. I wrap the soaking-wet sleeves of my blouse around his neck and kiss the side of his cheek as pure happiness floods my soul. "You're really here!"

"I'm really here."

"What are you doing here, Westly?" Art asks through his laughter.

West puts me down and turns toward his grandfather, drawing him close in a tight embrace. "I had to see my best friend Maggie on her twenty-eighth birthday," he explains, turning to me and winking in the charming way he often does.

"It's your birthday?" Art asks, mouth gaping wide.

"Yes," I say, gathering my blond tresses into my palm and squeezing the water out. But it has been years since West has come back to New England. Surely, he is not only here for my birthday. "But that *can't* be why you flew across the country."

I canvas his eyes for answers but come up empty. He sticks his hands in his back pockets and hesitates for a beat. "Catch up after work?"

I've known West long enough to know he has something important to tell me, and my stomach flips in a way I hadn't expected. "Yes," I affirm, turning toward Art. "But can we get out of the water now? I have an interview I need to get to."

West looks from me to his grandfather and back again, his eyes wide. "You haven't had your interview yet?"

I smile and throw my hands out by my sides. "Nope." I laugh because there is really nothing else to do but that.

"Yes." Art nods. "We can get out now, Maggie. But only because it's your birthday. Why didn't you tell me that in the first place?"

CHAPTER TWO- 2010

MAGGIE

I investigated my tired eyes in my bedroom mirror, determined to recover any kind of evidence that proved that the girl who stood before me was *not* the biggest loser in school. I knew I wasn't ugly, but I was also smart enough to understand that I was *not* pretty, not in the kind of way that my sister Jordan was pretty. Although she and I shared the same emerald-green eyes, *hers* seemed to sparkle in a way mine just couldn't. And even though we had both been blessed with the kind of blond hair that women spent hundreds of dollars for at the salon (Jordan's words, not mine), her golden tresses seemed to constantly appear velvety and smooth, while mine presented as a tangled and frizzy disaster.

I realized that the teenage years were destined to be brutal, but what was happening to me felt inhumane. It was one thing to be mistreated in school—but the public humiliation that came with the embarrassing and horrific Facebook and Myspace posts was almost too much to bear. I also understood that high school could be challenging, and kids would be mean, but then why didn't Jordan struggle? Jordan had it *all*. She'd made the varsity cheerleading team in the fall of her freshman year, and by sophomore year, she was dating the captain of the soccer team. She was inducted into the National Honor Society by junior year, and by the time she was a senior, she was awarded a dance scholarship to the Boston Conservatory at Berklee. It's no wonder she would never be able to understand me—nobody in my family could. And that is why I needed to complete the mission. I longed to fit in with the *only* group of people who ever accepted me… even if it meant breaking the law.

Honestly, I didn't have much to lose. I would be starting my senior year at York High in the fall, and the only academic accomplishment that seemed significant enough for a college resume was an award I received for a project that supported a local food pantry… and that was a *group* project. I attempted running cross country freshman year and broke my ankle during the first week of practice. I joined photography club last year due to my parents threatening to take my car away if I didn't find *some* after-school activity for my college applications. Apparently, binge-watching *Carolina Sands*, my favorite show on DVD, for hours on end didn't count as extracurricular. I was bored to tears when my first photography assignment consisted of taking pictures of the natural wonders around me… Kill. Me. Now.

I tried to fit in, really, I did. But nothing I did was working… until I met Grayson. The day I met Grayson Astor completely changed my life. I had been leaning on a stone bench, gaze focused on my camera—specifically, on the photos I had taken of a seagull perched on a rock in front of the Nubble Lighthouse. At first, I had assumed Grayson was part of an after-school club too. It didn't take long to realize that he was alone and, for whatever reason, wanted to talk to *me*. He smiled at me in a way that the other students couldn't be bothered to; it was like he cared that I existed.

"What are you doing?" he had asked, his voice warm and smooth. He was handsome, and I could feel blood rushing to my cheeks.

I adjusted my ponytail and smiled in the most confident way I knew how. "Photography club," I mumbled. "I'm supposed to be taking photos of the natural wonders around me."

"Sounds lame." He chuckled.

A ginormous laugh escaped from my soul, and for a moment, I was overly thankful for this person, whoever he was. "It is," I agreed. "It is *really* lame."

"I'm Grayson. Grayson Astor."

I nodded my head earnestly, like a fan meeting her favorite celebrity. "I'm Maggie Thatcher."

He studied me for a beat. "Follow me, Maggie Thatcher," he stated, a sudden seriousness in his voice.

"I… um…" my voice trailed off as he sprang up from the bench and marched briskly in the opposite direction of my classmates. It was then I noticed his thick black hair was tied back in a ponytail; I was suddenly very curious about him. I peeked over my shoulder at the supervising teacher and students, who were diligently taking pictures of birds, butterflies, and beach roses, and it was in that moment I decided for myself that I had discovered my own inspiration —Grayson Astor.

My new friend skipped effortlessly over the rocks of the Nubble, and I followed closely behind, the soles of my black Converse sneakers guiding me miraculously over each rock until he secured himself in a tiny cove. He plopped down on the ground, and I towered over him, studying him like I was cramming for a big test. He was quite handsome, older than me for sure, and although he wasn't clean-cut like the guys my sister brought home, he was attractive to me in a bad-boy rebellious sort of way, and for a moment, my heart started beating at a pace I only recognized from when I was forced to run sprints in gym class.

Grayson reached into his pocket and pulled out a rolled-up piece of something too small to be a cigarette, and I realized in that moment it was a joint.

"Weed?" I asked, my eyes wide.

"Here," he said as he lit it, and he took a puff, exhaled a large cloud of smoke, and passed it toward my awestruck face. "This is *my* natural wonder."

That had been a month ago, the day I met Grayson Astor. I later learned that he'd recently graduated from a nearby boarding school, one I had never heard of, but my knowledge of private schools in the area had been limited, to say the least. At first, our time together was spent in our little cutout cove down by the Nubble, smoking and staring up at the stars. Grayson was the first real friend I had ever known. If my parents had noticed my new recreational pastime, they didn't mention it. My mother even applauded me for the wonderful job I was doing in photography club. My teacher had emailed her, singing my praises. *Maggie has suddenly grown so creative*, she had written. *She quite possibly may have a future in photography... so lovely that she is finally feeling inspired.*

Nothing inspired me more than the night at the Nubble Lighthouse when Grayson and I had counted the stars. We were sprawled out on the grassy hill under the jet-black night sky. The tips of the grass tickled the back of my neck, and the dampness from the earth had begun saturating my legs and lower back, but I didn't mind one bit; Grayson Astor was holding my hand, and the emptiness that once encompassed my entire world began to melt away.

"What are you thinking about?" he had whispered.

I had been at a loss for words because I was overwhelmed with joy, the crisp night air, the twinkling stars, his breath against my cheek. I bit my lip and smiled at him and decided that in this moment, it was better to say nothing at all. He traced my nose with his pointer finger, then my cheek and my lips until he was holding my chin in his hand, and his lips met mine—my first kiss. It was everything that I had hoped it would be. The two of us, in the grass, our bodies intertwined under the Nubble's glow.

Our time together truly was wonderful at first. But then, he brought the *others,* and it wasn't just Grayson and me anymore. Lindsay, Grayson's half sister, was the first to crash our nights at the Nubble. Followed by his friends Brian and Samantha. They seemed to pop up one at a time, like pesky little rodents, arriving home from the same prep school, each one invading my happy little high with the only one I cared about, the only one who cared about me.

So there I was, one month later. I had kissed my mother and father goodbye, something I did each time I left the house. Only this time, the twist I felt in the pit of my stomach was almost too much to bear. I almost backed out of the mission entirely when my dad bent down, kissed my fore-head, and whispered a gentle "Happy seventeenth birthday, sweetheart. We are so proud of you."

I had searched his eyes for any sign of disappointment in me but came up empty. *I could bail on this whole thing,* I thought to myself. But it was too important. I needed to be with Grayson, and if I completed the mission, I would get to be one of them, and then I could see him as often as I wanted. The need to fit in and the desire to be with Grayson were enough to keep me moving forward with our plan.

I stuck the key in the ignition and drove away, leaving Windswept, our home in York Harbor, behind me. The large brown Victorian house towering high on the hill all but screamed, *Don't do it, Maggie! Come back!* But I rolled down the windows of my white Toyota Camry and allowed the comfort of the salty air to wash over me with gentle reassurance.

"How did I get myself into this?" I asked the darkness around me. But I knew the answer. It was Samantha who had given me the hardest time at first. It was no secret to any of us that she had a thing for Grayson. I had started to wonder if the rest of the group had a problem with Grayson and me being together, and it didn't take long before I realized that yes, they did have an issue with it, or they wouldn't be putting me through the initiation... they wouldn't be forcing me to complete the mission. To be part of their gang, I would need to complete the assigned tasks.

Grayson had shown up at my house out of nowhere the night he dropped the news. I had been completely surprised to see him standing at the front door of Windswept, as I didn't even realize he knew where I lived. We walked down the street through the darkness of the night into the Hartley Mason Reservation, and my insides all but exploded with anticipation when he took my hand and led me up the cliff walk. We had hiked, together, up the steep hill that bordered York Harbor Beach, and I paused for a moment to inhale the invigorating scent of low tide. But Grayson was on a mission of his own, and sightseeing was not in the cards.

"We don't have a lot of time," Grayson muttered, catching me off guard as he yanked my arm, somewhat forcefully, and we hunched down behind a cluster of trees. "We need to talk."

"What's going on?" I asked between breaths, more than disappointed that we would be talking and not kissing.

He peeked over his shoulder and leaned against the large oak tree as he grabbed my waist and pulled me close. I inched forward for a kiss, but he stopped me. "Listen carefully," he whispered, like an FBI agent confessing his secret identity. The seriousness of his expression scared me a bit, and the wild look in his eyes grew eerier against the moon's glow.

"What? What is it?"

"I like you, Maggie," he had started. "But there is a lot you don't know about me."

I pulled back in surprise. "Okay," I said between breaths, my quivering voice cutting through the sharpness of the silence. "What do you need to tell me?"

"I'm not that great of a guy, Maggie. I do things… bad things."

"Is this about the smoking? I'm cool with the—"

"No, Maggie. It's not the smoking. Look… I'm involved with some things that you don't need to be a part of. And us being together, it just isn't a good idea."

"What kinds of things?"

Our eyes locked, and I pleaded with my stare. *Don't do this*, I thought. *Don't break up with me, Grayson.*

"There is a group of us. I don't know how it started…"

I wrapped my arms around his neck and pulled him close to me, unable to resist twisting a strand of his long dark hair around my finger. "A group of you? I'm not sure I understand. Whatever it is, Grayson, we can work it out."

He pulled me close and squeezed me tighter than expected. "It happened at school last fall. I cheated on a few history tests, and one of the guys found out. They threatened to tell if I didn't complete… if I didn't complete a mission."

"A mission?"

"Yes, a mission. I know it sounds dumb, but I did it, and it was just… it was just awful."

"What did you do?" I had asked, my eyes wide.

He shook his head. "That doesn't matter. What matters is that it happened to all of us. Lindsay, Brian, and Samantha. They all completed missions too. And in turn, we had the protection of these kids at school; they had our backs.

But we made a pact… we would only allow certain people into the group. People who would complete missions with us."

"It sounds kind of like…" My voice trailed off.

"You can say it, Maggie. It sounds like a gang. Because it is one. I am in a gang."

There had been a rustling in the bushes and footsteps as Grayson pulled me down, practically on top of him, as a man and a woman walked past us up the Cliff Walk. Grayson lost his balance, and we toppled over, him landing on his back and me on top of him. I inhaled his sweet smell and tried with all my might to take in this moment. The thought of losing him turned my stomach in ways that were not comprehensible.

"I want to be with you," I whispered, pressing my body on top of his and pressing my lips to his. He kissed me back, and suddenly the idea of not being able to be together made me want him more than I had in the first place. "What do I need to do?" I kissed his forehead, his ear, and his lips again. "Give me a mission, Grayson."

I realized that breaking the law was not the best option. But at what point should a person sacrifice the only good thing they have felt in years only to take the high road? At what point should I settle for mean girls writing nasty messages on my locker and posting *LOSER* on my social media accounts? Especially when I had all I needed right in front of me.

So there I was on that Friday night, the night of my seventeenth birthday, only two days after my make-out session with Grayson in the woods of Hartley Mason Reserve, driving up the hill to the Nubble Lighthouse. I turned off my headlights, then my ignition, and checked the time on my cell—9:00 p.m. The Nubble Lighthouse stood high on a hill of emerald green under a starry sky. Its red glow lit up the water before me, revealing the massive waves that collided against the rocky shore.

"High tide... great," I whispered sarcastically. *"Just* what I need."

I leaned my head back against the headrest and closed my eyes. My head started to pound, and my stomach flipped and flopped. What if I got caught? Grayson insisted that this initiation was nothing compared to the missions they had all completed and that I was making this a big deal. But had they met *me*? Maggie Thatcher, the clumsy girl who fell down the stairs of the freshman building on the first day of school? The girl who was *always* chosen last in sports? The one who'd get caught the first time she broke any rule?

Yes, I needed to complete this mission. Taking my destiny into my own hands was critical; I would complete this challenge if it was the last thing I did. I sighed and stretched my arms overhead, landing my focus on the twinkling stars before me. I wondered how many stars there were in the sky. A million? A billion? More? I tried counting them, but my attention span failed me once again. Now wasn't the time to count the stars. Now all there was left to do... was wait.

CHAPTER THREE- 2010

WEST

This wasn't the first time I had flown from Arizona to Boston. I was nine years old the first time my father had hugged me goodbye at Gate C3 of American Airlines Flight 2229. He stuck a ten-dollar bill in my back pocket, secured my backpack around my shoulders, and sent me off with a flight attendant down a ramp that smelled like dirty feet and seemed to go on forever.

"Kiss Grandpa for me," he had called out. I could tell he was holding back tears, but I tried with all my might to ignore him. After all, I was a kid, and dads weren't supposed to cry. And if I looked back at him, I knew I would cry, too, and I just couldn't take that chance. I needed to be strong for both of us. But I couldn't shake the butterflies that had formed in the pit of my stomach and the emptiness that came with my unanswered questions. Why did Dad have to send me away?

Eight years later, there I was, finishing up a flight on the red-eye, sneaking a peek out my tiny window at the bluer-than-blue sky and the thin white cirrus clouds as we zoomed by. "Home" by Chris Daughtry serenaded my scattered thoughts and tired soul. I had a habit of reflecting on things that were completely out of my control, especially when on an airplane. Why did my father ship me off to live with Grandpa each summer? Simple. Because I didn't have a mother. What had happened to my mother? I wish I had an explanation. Because even though I had spent my entire life searching for an answer to this question, begging and pleading with my dad and grandfather to provide me any sort of information about her, neither one of them would budge.

"Why did Mommy leave?" I had often asked my dad. "Will I ever meet her?"

His responses left a lot to be desired. "None of that is important, Westly. The important thing is we have each other… you, me, and Grandpa."

I pouted and furrowed my brows. "Do you have a picture of her?"

"No, Westly," he scolded. "We don't have a picture."

"Can you tell me what she looked like?" I pleaded, still not able to get him to clarify if she was dead or alive.

"Look in the mirror, Westly," he muttered under his breath. "You look just like her."

I nodded, confirming what I had already expected. Even as a child, I could understand that my physical features could not have come from my father, Arthur Junior. We shared the same brown eyes, but my thick head of brunette hair looked nothing like his curly blonde tresses. Our skin tones and facial features were also much different—so much so the kids at school had asked about it once. But talking with my father about my mother would always come at a price. I learned quickly after that conversation that nothing good was going to come from asking about her. My father did an exceptional job raising me on his own, and I figured that I should quit while I was ahead. But when his career as a lawyer took off quicker than he had anticipated, he had no choice but to take Grandpa up on his offer to help out during the summer months.

I would be lying if I said that spending that first summer as a nine-year-old kid with Grandpa Art at WVC wasn't completely amazing, because it was. *Really* amazing. Not only did I have Grandpa's attention one hundred percent of the time, I had *everyone's* attention. Grandpa had been living in his own condo in the retirement wing of WVC, and every day with him was better than a trip to Disneyland.

Growing up in Arizona, trips to the beach were hard to come by. I had been a desert boy through and through. I could tell you all there was to know about Camelback Mountain, the long hilly mound of reddish-brown soil; what was breathtaking to some looked like silly gigantic anthills to me. I had grown accustomed to the hot dry days and the cool desert nights. So when I stuck my toes in the Atlantic Ocean with Grandpa that first summer, I was instantly hooked.

There I was, descending into Boston for the eighth summer in a row. I was not only excited to get back up on my surfboard and reunite with my elderly friends, but I was also starting to wonder if this might be my *last* summer trip to Maine. I would be starting my senior year of high school in the fall, and although I appreciated my time with Grandpa at Wells Valley Cove, I wasn't sure how realistic it would be to continue visiting him during my college years.

One wave at a time, I told myself, a philosophy that my grandfather had instilled in me from my first summer visiting him. It had been my first surfing lesson, and this desert boy was getting *rocked.* I had mastered prone position and the jump up on my board, but I couldn't quite get the timing right, and I experienced wipeout after wipeout, the saltwater rushing through my nose and stinging my throat like a thousand tiny razor blades.

"I don't want to fall again," I had cried out. "Can we stop? Please?"

"One wave at a time, Westly," he reassured. "Forget about that last one and focus on the next. You can do it."

"I can do it," I repeated back. And I did. The next wave was perfect. It flowed toward me like those I had only seen in movies. It rose out of the water, and was preparing to break right behind me.

"Paddle!" Grandpa called out. I had paddled my little heart out, felt the push of the foamy water beneath me, pushed myself up on my board... first my knee, then my feet... I was *surfing!*

"Yes!" Grandpa had called from the waist-deep ocean water. "Just like that!"

Eight years later, there I was, unbuckling my seat belt and reaching overhead for my carry-on, secretly hoping this wouldn't be my last visit to the East Coast. Because what had started as a strategy to help my single father with childcare had turned out to be the thing I looked forward to more than anything else in the world.

CHAPTER FOUR- NOW

MAGGIE

ONE MONTH BEFORE THE BIG DAY

I try to disregard the horrified expressions of those around me as I dash frantically down the Charles Gary Thatcher Wing of Wells Valley Cove's main activities center (named after my grandfather, of course) and into the gift shop. It has only been minutes since West and I plucked Art Young from the ocean and secured him back in assisted living, and I realize, as I scurry into the quaint little store, that I am leaving a trail of wet, sandy flip-flopped footprints behind me. "Sorry," I murmur somewhat under my breath. But I am too consumed with the mission before me: find something—*anything*—to wear to my interview. The one that started five freaking minutes ago.

I scan the gift shop and all its West Valley Retirement Cove souvenirs. Coffee mugs line the wall; hand-painted artifacts from sand dollars to Christmas ornaments stack the shelves. For a moment, my gaze stops short on a clam shell with a painting of the Nubble Lighthouse on its smooth surface. Even in the intensity of this moment, as I stand dripping wet in my skirt and blouse, I am shaken to the core as I recall that night back in 2010. That night at the Nubble Lighthouse when my life completely changed forever.

"What the *hell* did you do?"

I spin my head around, and my tangled saltwater-drenched hair whips my face. Seth. Freaking. Jenson. Just what I need. I make eye contact with him for a beat, only to notice quickly, as revealed by his flushed red cheeks and his gaping mouth, that he can see through my soaking-wet white blouse. I glance down at my chest quickly and try with all my might to ignore the fact that the outline of my bra is so apparent that I may as well be standing there topless.

"Work stuff," I state confidently as I push past Seth, who is already asking the cashier for a mop to wipe up the water I've deposited on the floor.

I grab a black Wells Valley Cove polo shirt and a pair of black sweatpants off the rack. The idea of sitting in front of the interview team in this attire suddenly makes me want to vomit. Regardless, I don't have any other choice. "Put this on my account, please," I instruct the cashier. She nods her head, and I bolt out of the store and toward my office, Seth trailing eagerly behind like my Labrador retriever, Finley, when he wants to go for a walk.

"I don't have time for this, Seth," I hiss, my stride growing bigger with every second. "I have my interview."

"You're going like *that?*"

"No," I state firmly. "I'm changing into these."

"Maggie—"

I fling my office door open, adrenaline pumping through my veins. "Talk later," I snap, slamming the door behind me. I rip the tags off my polo shirt and sweatpants and peel off my saturated skirt. My fingers tremble as I unbutton my blouse. "I can't believe I messed this up!" I shout to the empty room. But of course, I *can* believe it. It isn't the first significant life event I have screwed up, and it won't be my last. I fling my dirty clothes across the room, including my dripping under-wear and bra, and shimmy into my new outfit. I ignore the buzzing of my cell phone as text after text comes through, surely pertaining to the interview I am missing.

"I can't move any faster!" I shout again as I buckle the straps of my black Jimmy Choos, which look absurd paired with the black sweats. I button my suit coat and toss my tangled hair into a messy bun. I reach into my purse and grab my berry lipstick as I study my reflection in the mirror. "Could be worse," I mutter under my breath, applying my lipstick with ease. "Here goes nothing."

* * *

"KENDRA!" I shout as I fling open the door to the administrative wing. "Are they still in there?"

"Maggie? Maggie, are you wearing *sweatpants?*"

"Yes," I affirm like it's completely normal to style sweats with Jimmy Choos for your biggest interview *ever*. "Are they still in there?"

"Yes, they are ready for you."

She rises from her seat and opens the door to the confer-ence room. "Good luck," she whispers.

The faces of the interview panelists are familiar, which doesn't surprise me, as I have worked at WVC for over a decade. I strut in confidently, pretending that I am dressed for success, while the reality of the current situation is that I am walking into the biggest interview of my life not wearing any underwear.

"I'm very sorry I'm late."

They don't look thrown off by my less-than-impressive appearance, and I don't know whether I should feel relieved by this. On one hand, it could mean that they don't even notice, but on the flip side, it could mean they have gotten used to me, Maggie Thatcher—the one who screws everything up.

I study the familiar faces of the interview team, my father's being one of them, and I mentally prepare myself for the rapid-fire questions that will begin any moment now. *Just breathe,* I tell myself. *One wave at a time, Maggie. One wave at a time.*

CHAPTER FIVE- 2010

MAGGIE

I shifted uncomfortably in the driver's seat of my parked Toyota, wiping the beads of sweat from my palms onto my jeans. I glanced down at my cell phone and checked the time: 11:25 p.m. Only five more minutes until my plan would kick into action. Or, on the flip side, I had five more minutes to bail.

I closed my eyes and clenched my fists by my sides, my father's voice haunting me from the back of my mind. *Happy seventeenth birthday, sweetheart... We are so proud of you.* I shook my head from side to side and pulled my knees to my chest, fiddling with the laces of my black Converse. I imagined the disappointment on my father's face when he would realize that I was not his darling little sweetheart; I was not Jordan— I would never be her. I, Maggie Rose Thatcher, was about to be initiated into a *gang*.

The ringing from my cell phone startled me. It was Grayson Astor calling, right on schedule. I swiped open the call and had the phone to my ear before a second ring. "Grayson," I said, pronouncing his two-syllable name like it would fill my lungs with air. "Grayson... I-I... don't think I can—"

"It's perfectly normal to be scared, Maggie." His voice sounded smooth but firm. "You need to do this... It's the only way."

"I know," I moaned. "But I'm going to get caught. I *always* get caught, Grayson."

"Take a deep breath. This is a piece of cake. We've *all* done it."

I tightened my jaw and held my breath, staring up at the stars in the sky. "And if I don't?"

Grayson exhaled a long and frustrated sigh and was silent for a beat. We shared a moment of understanding during the extended quiet between us.

"Grayson? If I don't do this?" I whispered again into my phone, hopeful that maybe his feelings for me superseded the initiation code put in place by his friends. "Couldn't we figure out some other way? Like pretend that I pulled it off or something?"

"It's not an option, Maggie. It's eleven thirty. It's time for you to go."

* * *

I ADJUSTED my backpack over my shoulders and secured my blond ponytail through the back of my baseball cap. There was no turning back now. I canvased the parking lot of the Nubble Lighthouse just as Grayson had instructed. The restaurant was closed for the evening, and there were no tourists in sight—typical for a weeknight that time of year, but it still felt eerie and lonesome. I quietly wished for someone, anyone, to appear out of nowhere and be my excuse for bailing on the mission. But nobody was around... just me.

I had practiced scooting down the rocky hill on my

bottom earlier that week, but that had been in the daylight. My lanky arms and legs flipped and flopped over the large rocks as I shimmied my way across them in the darkness, repeatedly scraping and banging my elbows against the rough surfaces. "Ouch," I whispered in the blackness of the night, considering for a moment whether I should go back to my car and drive home. But I had already come this far, and at that point, climbing back up that hill seemed just as impossible as completing the mission ahead of me.

For a moment, I peered behind me at the parking lot above, relieved to find that I was still alone. I turned back toward the Nubble Lighthouse and crept slowly to the edge of the rocks. The lighthouse appeared gigantic from this angle, and I realized that although I grew up in York, I had never had the luxury of experiencing it in this way—alone, on its hill, shining down on me with its red glow. A strong sensation of guilt struck a nerve somewhere inside me. The people of Cape Neddick and York, Maine, cared deeply about their lighthouse, and what I was about to do would be a serious sign of disrespect. Sure, lighthouses were meant to warn incoming ships of rocky shorelines, but was this one warning me, Maggie Thatcher... to go home?

I shook my head and decided that I wouldn't quit. There was too much at stake. I closed my eyes and pictured the way Grayson kissed me passionately just nights before. The torture in his eyes as he explained we could not be together. I would not be bailing on the mission. Instead, I studied the challenge before me. I needed to cross over the gigantic chasm to successfully trespass onto Nubble Island. During low tide, this would have been difficult, to say the least, but amid high tide, it was dangerous... especially in the darkness.

The plan had been to wade across the water, but the tide was too high for that. Grayson had suggested I take the tiny white dinghy boat—the same cute little boat I had taken photos of for photography club just a few days earlier—but there were no oars. I was a strong swimmer, and I would get myself over to Nubble Island without the boat. However, that would mean leaving most of my cargo behind.

I dropped my backpack behind me and quickly began removing my shoes and shimmying out of my jeans. I took off my baseball cap and pulled my T-shirt over my head and tossed it on the ground. It was just me, Maggie Thatcher, standing before one of the most beautiful landmarks I had come to know, in the stillness of the night, in my favorite purple two-piece bathing suit. "What am I doing?" I asked the lighthouse. I waited a moment, somewhat expecting it to answer me. But of course, it couldn't; instead, my eyes landed on a *NO TRESSPASSING* sign just a few feet from where I dropped my bag. I looked away and, for a moment, pretended it didn't exist.

I rummaged through my backpack and pulled out my waterproof disposable camera, pausing only for a moment before tucking it away in the back of my bathing suit bottoms. I checked around me one more time, eager for a way out of this mess, but there was no way out. I inhaled and exhaled, completely aware of my trembling knees and racing heart.

The mission had sounded simple at first: cross over from the parking lot of the Nubble Lighthouse onto Nubble Island and take a photograph of myself in front of the lighthouse with my disposable camera. But as I faced the water under the darkness of the night sky, it didn't feel so easy anymore. The bottoms of my feet ached as I stepped over what I imagined were tiny pieces of rocks and shells. The frigid ocean water stung my legs as I sank farther in. I waded as far in as I could before it was just too deep and I needed to swim.

I took a deep breath, adjusted the camera in my bathing suit, glanced up in the direction I needed to go, and dove into an oncoming wave. The water was bone-chilling, but my adrenaline was elevated. Although I knew I was supposed to feel something, I really couldn't feel much. My strokes were long and steady, and my breathing was controlled. I silently thanked my parents for years of swimming lessons, and I tried with all my might to forget about the sea creatures that could have been lurking in the darkness; the tips of my toes tingled in anticipation of the unknown.

I breathed a sigh of relief when my feet could reach the bottom again. I crawled to shore, kicking through the seaweed, exhausted from my journey across the chasm. But my adventure had only just begun. The hill supporting the lighthouse was steeper than expected, but I found the ramp Grayson had mentioned. I crawled up the ramp, slipping from time to time and shaking from the crisp night air until I felt grass between my toes, and I realized I had done it. I had made it to Nubble Island. *Don't celebrate yet,* I warned myself. I paused for a moment, taking in the view from this side of the lighthouse, and then reminded myself I didn't have time to waste. If someone did see me trespassing, I would only have so long to get back.

I had only one thing left to do: take a photograph of myself on the front steps of the lighthouse. To do this, I would need to run up the hill under the glow of the Nubble and use the flash on my camera, which could draw attention to me if I wasn't careful. I took a deep breath and sprinted toward the front porch, but the grass under my wet feet was not forgiving, and I fell... hard. The camera flew, and I reached for it in desperation, therefore allowing my body to hit the ground without the support of my hands. I slid across the front lawn of the Nubble on my bare stomach, unable to catch my breath, feeling like I had been kicked in the gut. I scurried around on the ground, frantically trying to find my camera but coming up empty. And then I saw them. The lights—the red and blue lights of police cars flashing at me from across the chasm by where I parked my car. I army-crawled on my elbows until I was safely tucked away behind a tiny red shed, trying very unsuccessfully to catch my breath and hopeful that they were there for someone else... *anyone* else.

"Maggie Thatcher," the officer called from a megaphone of some sort.

I grimaced, leaned against the shed, pulled my knees to my chest, and closed my eyes. *This isn't happening*, I told myself.

"Maggie Thatcher... we know you are out there."

CHAPTER SIX- 2010

WEST

*I*t had been less than a week since I'd settled in with Grandpa at Wells Valley Cove, just as I had done so many times over the years. As I strolled down the carpeted hallway toward the Marjorie Ruth Thatcher Dining Hall, a familiar wave of nostalgia washed over me. What had once started as a stretch of private retirement condos on a private beach in Wells, Maine, had been developed into what felt like its own city.

Growing up in a retirement community had its perks. I was the only child amongst what felt like hundreds of senior citizens, and they *loved* me. Of course, my favorite thing to do with Grandpa was surf; the water was his favorite place to be. But it wasn't just the beach that kept me entertained— Grandpa had friends. Friends that liked to play cards. By my tenth birthday, I could hold my own in a game of War, and by the time I was twelve, I could play 45s in my sleep, and by my fourteenth birthday, I mastered the game of poker.

I found my usual table in the dining hall, a corner booth by the window overlooking the beach, and peeked at my watch. Grandpa would be meeting me for dinner any moment. I reached across the table for a menu, eager to see what the specials were for the evening. I remembered for a moment that first summer I came to live at WVC and chuckled to myself because I had convinced the head chef to add Kraft mac 'n' cheese to the daily menu.

A gentle hand on my shoulder interrupted my thoughts. "Hi, Westly, dear."

I glanced up from my menu and smiled. "Hi, Mrs. Jones, how are you this evening?" I kissed her hand like Grandpa had taught me to do many years ago.

"I'm good, dear. Are you meeting your grandfather for dinner?"

"Yup, he should be here any second."

Mrs. Jones reached forward and placed her hands on my shoulders. "You are such a good boy, coming to visit him every summer. You keep him young, you know."

I nodded and smiled, convinced she was referring to the fact that Grandpa seemed to be getting older and grumpier by the second. It wasn't until the passing of my grandmother, Gloria, that my grandfather moved into the retirement community. Mrs. Jones and many of the other residents pointed out often that I served as a positive distraction for Grandpa.

"It was nice to see you, dear. I'm glad you're here."

"Nice to see you, too, Mrs. Jones."

She scurried over to her usual table of a group of ladies her age, and I laughed to myself, thinking that they were the older version of the girls at my high school.

"Westly," Grandpa stated as he sat down across from me. He wore his usual Hawaiian-style top and khaki dress pants. "Anything good on the specials?"

"That depends on what you consider good. It looks like tonight is the pot roast special."

Grandpa paused for a beat and grimaced, like the term

"pot roast" was a curse word. "I suppose I will stick with pizza."

"Sounds like a plan."

Grandpa flagged down one of the servers, and he ordered his regular pepperoni pizza. He entertained the waitress with his usual predictable jokes and playful banter. I smiled, feeling nostalgic once again. Grandpa also ordered a glass of red wine and me a Roy Rogers. I didn't have the heart to tell him that I gave up drinking Roy Rogers when I was about thirteen years old, because for a moment, it sounded like the best thing in the entire world.

I RAN my fingers through my thick brown hair and sighed. Grandpa's balcony was one of my favorite spots at WVC. The breeze off the coast was invigorating, and the stars in the night sky twinkled brighter than those back home. I glanced over at Grandpa, who was resting comfortably in a lounge chair, and I was sure he must have been asleep, but he wasn't. He was gazing up at the stars just as I was.

"What are you thinking about?" I asked him.

He was silent for a moment but then cleared his throat. "Life," he whispered. "Thinking about life. Life and love," he admitted, a bit bashfully.

I squirmed in my seat, a bit uncomfortable with this topic. "So… like… you are thinking about Grandma Gloria?" I had never met my grandmother, as I was born and raised in Arizona and my grandparents never made the trip out there while she was, well… while she was alive.

"I loved your grandmother, yes." He argued more than answered. "I… I just think about a lot of things when I sit out here."

"I've never been in love," I admitted.

Grandpa turned toward me and sighed. "Love is a funny thing. If you ask me, there is a difference between love and life."

"What do you mean?"

Grandpa cleared his throat. "I mean—I just mean that just because you love someone… and they might very well be your soulmate, doesn't mean you get to…" He shook his head and stopped himself midsentence.

"Do you believe in soulmates?"

"You sure are asking a lot of questions tonight, aren't you?"

"Sorry," I mumbled. "It's just that… Dad doesn't talk about this kind of stuff. And I know you have been in love."

"I do believe in soulmates. For a long time, I believed that we only each get one soulmate. But then…" His voice trailed off again. "It's funny, isn't it? I feel like I was just having this conversation with your father… Why, I feel like it was only moments ago that your father was a senior in high school. Where on Earth does the time go?"

I turned toward him and studied his expression. Although he was with me in a physical sense, I could tell that emotionally, he was on an entirely different planet. He was lost in his memories. His smile was gleeful, like a child's on Christmas morning.

"Why can't we talk about my mother?" I blurted out, faster and louder than I had meant to.

Grandpa's eyes narrowed, and his nose scrunched up to his eyeballs. "It's time to call it a night," he said firmly. And with that, he stood from his chair, grabbed his glass of wine, and left me there on his balcony in the darkness, wondering why on Earth talking about my mother would be so off-limits.

"I'm heading out for a walk," I called to him in the darkness. I paused and waited for a moment for a response, any kind of response, and then sighed. Seventeen years of asking about my mother and seventeen years of being left alone on a balcony, wondering what kind of person she must have been to leave in the first place because the mere mention of her name did more harm than good.

CHAPTER SEVEN- NOW

MAGGIE

ONE MONTH BEFORE THE BIG DAY

I squeeze by a crowd of tourists, all of them eager to get a prime spot at the piano bar. The Sand Dollar Bar and Grille on Short Sands Beach has become a favorite spot for West and me over the years, and apparently, it has become quite the spot for *everyone*. I scan the room for West, still recovering from the shock of his arrival. I spot him, seated in the back of the room at the bar, and breathe a heavy sigh of relief. He is *home*.

He is making small talk with Chris, the bartender, and is already sipping a glass of red wine, his drink of choice, and I notice that he has already ordered me a glass of white. "Hey!" I sing as I drop my purse on the chair next to him.

"Maggie, you made it! And you don't look like a drowned rat anymore."

I glanced down at my jean skirt and favorite tank and nudge him playfully as I take my seat next to him, thankful that I had the opportunity to go home and get cleaned up prior to our night out. "It was one hell of a day—that's for sure." I sip my wine before sitting down, and I can't stop smiling at him. *He's like a freaking glass of wine*, I think to myself. *West Young has managed to get finer with age.*

"What's the smile for?"

"You!" I shriek. "You're actually *here*." I reach over and wrap my arms around his neck, inhaling the familiar smell of his cologne.

He smiles in the charming way he does. I study him again and shake my head in disbelief. Westly Young is *home.*

"How long has it been?" Chris inquires. "Since you two have seen each other?"

"It's been about…" His voice trails off, and I realize he has absolutely no idea how long it has been since he's been back.

"About five years," I finish for him. "But who's counting?" I add a wink and a shrug.

"Five years, man?" Chris asks. "That's a long time. You two must have a lot of catching up to do."

"We sure do," I agree, checking over the menu.

"Nachos?" West asks me.

"Of course," I reply, as they are my favorite. I study West and notice that he has been working out. His arm muscles are more defined than I remember. He's the same West I know inside and out, but he somehow seems… I don't know… different.

"Well, we will take the nachos," West tells Chris. "Hold the sour cream."

"Is that an allergy or a preference?"

Speaking of preference... I think, sipping my wine and silently screaming at myself to *stop* checking out my best friend. "Just a preference," I answer. "I don't like sour cream."

ABOUT AN HOUR and two more glasses of wine later, with some food in my stomach, I am finally able to laugh about my day without crying. Although West is giving me a hard time about showing up to my interview with soaking-wet hair and in sweatpants, deep down, I can tell he is thankful that I helped his grandfather... again.

"So, where are you staying, anyways?" I ask in between bites of my salad.

"Anderson Cottage," he responds. "First floor. Love that place."

I nod in agreement. "Art's old stomping grounds."

"That's right. Speaking of Grandpa—" he starts, stops, then starts again. "Does he seem to be getting worse?"

I dab my mouth with my napkin and take a sip of wine. "What do you mean, *worse?*"

He raises his eyebrows and narrows his stare. "You know what I mean, Mags."

My shoulders stiffen, and I gather my hair over my shoulder. "I mean... he's definitely getting *old.*"

West nods, and for a moment, I feel sorry that I even said anything. I hate to see him sad, especially when it comes to his grandfather. He shifts uncomfortably in his seat, and I can tell before his next word is spoken that he is going to change the subject. "So, did your interview end up going okay?"

I wince and shrug my shoulders. "I mean, as good as it could have gone, considering I swam there."

West laughs, and for a second, I think his wine will come out of his nose. "I really *have* missed you, Maggie."

I begin to smile, thankful for this acknowledgment, but I stop myself in my tracks. Because no matter how badly I want my friendship with West to be more, I know in my heart it will never happen... it *can't* happen. "Another glass of wine, please, Chris," I shout over the singing of the drunken tourists that surround us.

West doesn't release me from his stare, no matter what I

do to try to shrug off his sudden confession. I reach into my purse and locate my lipstick, and I continue applying it until my third glass of wine is securely within reach.

"Maggie," he starts again. "I said I missed you. Did you miss me?"

I rub my tired eyes with my fingers and let out a frustrated sigh. "Of course I missed you," I admit. "But I guess I was getting okay with the fact that text messages, FaceTime, and social media are just how it is going to be for us."

He gently places his hand on my shoulder, and his touch feels warm against my skin. "You're my best friend, Maggie."

"I know," I affirm. "Life just gets in the way, I guess." I take another sip of wine, and the past five years seem to flash through my mind at a billion miles per hour. I had planned trips to Arizona to visit West, but my responsibilities at WVC and commitment to my master's degree were overwhelmingly time-consuming. West had intended to visit during the summers, but after he got accepted to law school, it was like he was sucked into this black hole and couldn't come up for air. It's true; we got used to a long-distance friendship. And in my mind, that was better than nothing... especially because our relationship will never be more.

The piano music comes to an abrupt stop, and West smiles in that overly playful way he sometimes does.

"I have a surprise for you."

I gasp. "You didn't!"

He laughs and shakes his head. "Oh, I *so* did."

I spin around and face the crowded room before me as the piano player points in my direction and grins. "A big birthday shout-out to Maggie Thatcher on her twenty-eighth birthday!"

I smile the fakest smile possible while a crowd of tourists belts "Happy Birthday" to me at the top of their lungs, and West grabs my hand and spins me around and shows me off.

He pulls me close and dips me, and I have no choice but to play along.

"Want to take a walk?" he whispers in my ear. I nod because not only do I hate my birthday but because it is getting increasingly difficult to hear him over the crowd. I drop a handful of cash on the bar, and West hands it back to me.

"Thank you for dinner," I say as I gather my things and prepare for our walk, knowing deep down that West Young doesn't just fly across the country to say hello to his friends and family. There is something he needs to talk to me about, face-to-face, and my stomach begins to flip as I brace for impact, anticipating the conversation we are about to have. West has something to tell me—and I'm not going to like it.

CHAPTER EIGHT- 2010

MAGGIE

*W*ells Valley Cove and Retirement Center was established in 1980 as an average retirement community, an elegant stretch of apartments lining a private beach in Wells, Maine. That was, however, until my father, Gary Thatcher, purchased the property in 1999 and converted it into what I have always referred to it as the City of Old People. Of course, my father disagreed with this language, insisting that the success of his investment and clever use of his inheritance far exceeded such a feather-brained title. I had rolled my eyes at my father, like teenagers often do, and agreed cheerfully that I would change my wording and declared Wells Valley Retirement Cove the City of Senior Citizens.

Of course, I was being absurd; WVC was not only a gorgeous facility, but it was also rated in the top five retirement communities and assisted living centers in New England every year since 2003. What set it apart from similar facilities was not only its affordable beachfront location but also its ability to house nursing home patients, assisted living residents, and an entire independent retirement community.

Maybe it was because WVC encompassed my father's attention for the entire duration of my existence, or maybe it was because I would never be known as *just* Maggie Thatcher—I was Gary Thatcher's daughter—that when it came to WVC, I avoided it like the plague… that was, until that summer. Because it turns out that when you trespass onto private property such as Nubble Island, and you get caught red-handed, you end up getting in trouble with the law. And when you get in trouble with the law and you are not yet eighteen… it turns out you get sentenced to community service. And when your father runs a massive retirement and assisted living facility with a top-notch community service program… you get stuck volunteering there for six months.

It wasn't that I had better things to do, because I didn't. I was grounded for the rest of my existence, according to my parents—the perfect way to begin the summer leading into my senior year. My failure to complete the mission onto Nubble Island had been mortifying, to say the least. I basically handed the kids at school ammunition for my humiliation on a silver platter. But reliving the worst choice of my entire life on my Facebook page was not the worst part. The toughest pill to swallow was that I was sure it was Samantha who sold me out. And if Grayson knew about it, he did nothing to stop it. Did it really matter anyway? Even if I was allowed to see him again, it didn't seem like he was interested. I had failed to complete the mission. That was me… Maggie Thatcher, the failure.

"You seem to be getting the hang of things, all right," Mary, my supervisor, encouraged.

"I guess," I replied, feeling a bit annoyed that Mary felt the need to pay so much attention to me. After all, it had been a week since my training. I gathered the dirty dishes from table seven and stacked them on top of each other.

"Have the residents been kind to you?" she asked, clearly an effort to make small talk.

"Yup."

"That's good. They are all pretty much well-behaved."

"Good to know." I adjusted my blond ponytail and positioned the stack of dishes on my tray.

"There are some you might need to watch out for," she started. "Loraine from assisted living is approaching eighty-eight years old. Her bark is worse than her bite for sure."

I studied her for a beat and wondered why on Earth she felt the need to talk so much. She tucked her short black hair behind her ear, and if she noticed my aggravation, she ignored it.

"Of course," she sang, "Paul Richardson from independent living has been known to flirt from time to time. Be sure to report any inappropriate behavior directly to me... or, of course, your father."

"Uh-huh," I replied, at this point completely checked out. I wiped my hands on my apron and reached for my tray.

"Oh, and Westly Young—you will need to watch out for him. He's been here for years... nothing but trouble. Poor Rodger Santos lost fifty dollars to him in a game of poker last night. The guy shows *no* mercy."

What kind of name is Westly? I thought to myself. "I can handle them," I spat, more firmly than I meant to.

Mary placed a gentle hand on my shoulder. "You really are doing a great job, Maggie. I will be sure to tell your parents how quickly you have picked this up."

I tightened my jaw as the blood rushed to my cheeks in embarrassment, as being praised for completing simple tasks sent me into a spiral of insecurity. "Thanks," I muttered under my breath. "It's really not that hard." I lifted the tray of dishes and slumped forward, off balance.

She placed a reassuring hand on my shoulder. "Compliments are the biggest form of flattery," she lectured as if she were my mother. "It's okay to smile and just say thank you."

Mary followed me into the kitchen, and I chewed on my lower lip, determined to keep any disrespectful comments to myself, as Mary and her husband Tim were close friends of my mother and father's. I wiped my hands on my apron and made eye contact with Mary, and there was no denying the seriousness in her eyes. Surely, she was just as disappointed in me as my parents were. "Thank you!" I said faux enthusiastically, convinced that there was no way Mary would have the common sense to pick up on my sarcasm. "I'm going to get back to work now."

* * *

LATER THAT NIGHT, after I wiped down the dining hall tables and hung up my apron, I decided to go for a walk on the beach, something I hadn't done since my first night at WVC. Since the failed mission at the Nubble, I hadn't had a ton of time to myself. My parents had watched me like a hawk, and any free time that would have been mine was spent hanging with Jordan. They probably figured if I hung out with her long enough, I would catch her perfection, like some people catch a cold or the flu.

The private beach of WVC was peaceful at night. I enjoyed the serenity of the dark ocean water as it glistened under the moonlight. I had noticed that most of the residents spent time at the beach after lunch and before dinner. The independent living tenants were allowed out anytime after sunrise and before sunset, while the assisted living residents had rigid and structured schedules. This was information I had learned during my tour of WVC on my first day.

"What about the nursing home patients?" I had asked Sandra, my tour guide.

"What about them?"

"When do they get to swim?"

"They don't."

I had frowned and thought about this for a moment, and it didn't seem fair. I wondered for a moment just how terrible it must feel to have your freedom taken away. Would it be worse than being grounded? Worse than being betrayed by the only friends I had? I decided that yes, being locked up inside with little to no opportunity to inhale the salty air and dip your toes in the icy Atlantic was probably one of the worst things that could happen to a person. I needed the beach like I needed air.

I paused for a moment and stared out at the horizon. The water seemed to go on for miles—what I could see of it, anyway. The reflections of the stars on the dark expanse glistened and sparkled like glitter. As cool water splashed up onto my shorts, I was surprised to realize that I had wandered into the ocean and was now standing in it knee-deep, consumed by my daydreams.

"Nice night for a swim?"

I spun around, startled, and squinted my eyes toward the direction of the voice. "Who's there?" I called.

He approached me slowly, his hands in the back pockets of his jeans. "Westly," he started. "But my friends call me West."

His smile caught my attention first. His perfectly straight and whiter-than-white teeth gleamed at me in a larger-than-life sort of way. He kicked through the water, moving closer to where I stood. "Oh," I chuckled. "I've been warned about you."

He laughed, and a wave of calmness soothed my soul. "Oh, really? I thought I had a pretty good reputation around here."

Our eyes locked, and for the first time in years, I felt as though I was alive. "Something about a poker game," I started, surprised by my sudden confidence. "Rodger Santos and his retirement fund... will never be the same." I frowned and shook my head like a parent disappointed in a child, something I knew a little too much about.

He took a couple of steps closer. "I grew up playing cards here with my grandpa."

"So that's why you're here?" I asked. "Visiting?"

He rubbed his hand through his velvety dark hair. "Something like that... Do you work here?"

I peered down at my khaki shorts and black WVC polo shirt and nodded. "Something like that." I winked. "I'm Maggie. Maggie Thatcher." Our eyes remained locked as he took my hand in his.

"It's nice to meet you, Maggie Thatcher. I hope to see you around sometime."

* * *

THE NEXT TWO weeks went by quickly. The name Grayson Astor was far from my mind. Every day, I went to work at WVC and waited tables, and each night, West and I would walk on the beach. I quickly learned that his grandfather was Art Young, one of the independent residents. West had been flying out from Arizona each year since he was nine years old to spend the summers with him. What had started out as an arrangement to help his father with childcare had ended up being an extremely positive experience for him and his grandfather.

I would be lying if I said I didn't think about West Young

every second of the day. I had even confided in Jordan about him, which is something I never did—ever.

"What is he like?" she had shrieked when I mentioned his name.

"He's handsome, for sure."

"No way… Maggie! This is so exciting. Tell me about him."

I paused for a moment, considering this. What was there to say, really? He was the soul of a seventy-year-old man trapped in the body of a young Ian Somerhalder? "He's cool," I had muttered under my breath.

There we were, West and me, walking along the private beach, the sun just beginning to set. The sky was tickled with various shades of pinks and purples and blues when suddenly, West stopped short, tucked his hands in his pockets, and looked at the ground. "Is everything okay?" I had asked. The tide was out, and my feet sank into the muck as the frigid wet sand caved around my toes.

"Oh, yeah." He smiled. "I was just… I was just going to ask you something, and I didn't want it to be weird."

I adjusted my ponytail and placed my hands on my hips. "What could be weird?" I giggled. "It's just me."

We continued walking, closer together than normal, and I found myself staring at his footsteps in the sand, wondering what on Earth West Young was going to ask me.

He stopped again, as if reading my mind, and for a moment, my breath was caught in my throat. The smile on his face against the colorful sky and setting sun was enough to make me forget about everything… everything from the bullying at school to my screw-up at the Nubble. Even my time with Grayson Astor was a distant memory. "I was wondering… if you wanted to maybe get some pizza on Short Sands tomorrow night?"

My heart sank. Of course I wanted to get pizza with West.

I would die to get pizza with West. But the fact remained that I was very much grounded. "I would love to." I sighed. "But I'm currently grounded."

He exhaled and laughed, and for a moment, I could sense just how nervous he was. "Grounded?"

"Yeah," I nodded. "I'm grounded for the summer."

He laughed, and I realized he thought I was kidding. "So yes, then?"

I punched him playfully in the arm. "I'm serious." I giggled. "I'm really grounded, but I... I want to hang out. Could you maybe bring the pizza here?"

* * *

THE NEXT NIGHT, after the dinner shift, West and I sat perched on a blanket overlooking low tide, pizza in hand. West wore his jeans rolled up at the knees with a white dress shirt. I had never seen his hair with gel in it before, and he smelled like Old Spice; I wondered if he'd borrowed it from his grandfather.

"So, tell me," he said between bites. "What exactly does one do to get grounded for an entire summer?"

I grimaced and threw my arms up over my head. "Are you really going there?"

He laughed and nodded his head. "Oh, I'm going there."

I ditched my empty paper plate by my side and hugged my knees to my chest, wishing more than anything that I'd had the opportunity to wear something, anything, other than my tan shorts and black polo. "If I tell you, you are going to run away screaming."

West clapped his hands and laughed. "So this is going to be good, then?"

"I got caught up with the wrong crowd, I guess you could say." I bit my lip and hoped he would let me off the hook.

"And?" he asked, gesturing with his hands for more information.

I pressed my palm to my forehead. "I... I trespassed. Onto Nubble Island."

"The Nubble Lighthouse? Wow, that's... I don't even live here, and I know what a big deal that is."

I nodded my head. "It was stupid. I shouldn't have done it."

An hour later, I had told him the entire story of Grayson and the Prep School Gang. He listened, wide-eyed, as the sun set around us and the beach grew more and more vacant. We were lying down on our sides as we talked, and for the first time in my life, I felt like I'd found a piece of myself that was missing.

"So you are one hundred percent grounded, then. No going out with friends... only community service and home?"

"That's right," I said with a sigh.

"Did they take your cell phone? Can you watch TV?" he asked, still wide-eyed.

I snickered. "No, they didn't take my cell phone. They like to know where I am. And as far as TV, I don't watch much of it. Except I do like to binge *Carolina Sands* on DVD, and they didn't take that from me—thank God."

West threw his head back and cackled. "*Carolina Sands*? That's still around?"

I punched him playfully in the arm. "All twelve seasons!"

"That's the soap opera with Jon Simmons and Tara Lemur, right?"

I giggled. "First of all, it isn't a soap opera. And yes, it is with Jon Simmons, Tara Lemur, and my favorite of all time, Silvia Flores. It truly is the greatest show ever. It's like my comfort food, I swear."

West nodded as if understanding. "Well, I'm glad for your sake you didn't lose TV."

"So, since we are telling juicy secrets… why do you come visit your grandfather every year? Where are your parents?" His expression turned from soft to hard, and I instantly regretted asking such a question. "It's okay," I started. "You don't have to—"

He held his hand up and shook his head. "No, it's okay. I just don't really talk about that a lot."

"Then forget I brought it up."

"My father needed help… raising me. So he flew me out here when I was nine years old. It just kind of turned into a tradition."

"So, your dad… he's a single father?" I chose my words carefully.

West nodded his head in agreement. "I don't know who my mother is. I don't know if she is alive or dead. Every time I try to talk to my father or grandfather about her, it's like I am initiating a world war." He spoke quickly, and I couldn't help but notice the relief in his eyes when he finally released the information.

"That's… that's awful."

I sat up and crisscrossed my legs, thinking for a moment just how miserable that must have been for him. He sat up, too, and surprised me by resting his head on my shoulder. I inhaled, allowing the smell of his hair to consume me. I closed my eyes and rested my head on his.

We lay there, appreciating the silence, while the day turned to night and the stars made their debut in the sky. I started counting the little glimmers of light, and for a moment, my heart sank as I remembered Grayson and our nights together. I felt played, naïve to think that I knew anything about him after only a short couple of weeks. I wondered if he was somewhere by the Nubble, smoking a joint with his gang or even worse… initiating someone new into their group. I also wondered about West and how hard it must have been for him not knowing who his mother was. I said a silent prayer for him in hopes that he would get the answers he was looking for, then I inhaled the scent of Old Spice and said another for myself. If there was any possible way that I could have another night like this with West Young, then I would be the happiest girl alive.

"It's getting late," West whispered in my ear.

"It is."

"I wish we had a camera. It was our first night together, and I feel like such an important occasion should be documented."

"Oh yeah?" I giggled. "Our first night together, eh?"

"Knock it off," he teased.

I reached into my bag and rummaged through my belongings. "I have a camera," I said.

"Really?"

"Yeah. You are looking at York High School's newest photography club president."

He chuckled and took the camera from my hands. "You are going to have to show me how to turn it on."

After a few flicks of some switches, West Young had my digital camera on and flipped around in hopes of capturing a selfie of the two of us. The flash was bright, and my heart fluttered as we smiled and posed.

"Will you share those with me?" he asked.

"Of course. Are you on Myspace or Facebook?"

He stared at me blankly, shaking his head. "I guess I'm not too big on social media."

"I'll print them," I offered. "I'll print them and bring them tomorrow."

"Same time, same place?" he asked without missing a beat.

"Same time, same place."

CHAPTER NINE- 2010

WEST

Out of all my trips to West Valley Cove, I never in a million years would have thought I would make a friend under the age of sixty years old, let alone someone that I liked. And although this came out of nowhere and was very much unexpected, I liked Maggie Thatcher, a lot.

I had confided in Grandpa about her, and he did his research. I told him that wasn't necessary, that we were just friends, but he checked into her anyway. Turned out her father owned the establishment, just as she had mentioned. Grandpa seemed happy for me, to say the least. When I told him that I would be seeing her again, he gave me all sorts of embarrassing lectures about the birds and the bees, holding the door, and of course, telling her she's beautiful.

I had rolled my eyes because our friendship was new and we were not even permitted to leave the facility, her being grounded and all. But as I sprawled our blanket down on the sand of the private beach for the third night in a row, I couldn't wait to see her. So you could imagine my surprise when she wasn't on time like she usually was. I glanced at my watch and realized that she was running thirty minutes later than normal. I wondered to myself what would be keeping her. It was also at that moment I realized that I hadn't seen her earlier in activities or in the dining hall at night. I grew worried about Maggie and realized that I hadn't seen her at all that day.

I pulled out my cell phone and dialed her phone number. We had exchanged numbers the previous night, which I was relieved about because in less than one month, I would be back in Scottsdale, Arizona. She didn't answer her phone, and I decided not to leave a message. Instead, I lay down on my back on my blanket and watched the sunset alone, pondering the big things like I usually did in moments like these—my mother, for starters—and hoping that Maggie was okay. I didn't know her too well, but I knew her well enough to know that it wasn't like her to bail on anything... especially on us.

* * *

I AWOKE the next morning to my grandfather standing over me. He hovered over the couch in his white T-shirt and boxer shorts, staring like a scientist checking on an experiment. "Westly," he huffed. "Westly, you have a visitor."

I shot up on the couch, sitting and running my hands over my face. "A visitor?" I asked, confused. "What time is it, Grandpa?"

"West," Maggie cried. "I'm *so* sorry. I did... I did something terrible. Just terrible."

Maggie stood at the door of Grandpa's apartment, tears streaming down her cheeks. I glanced at the clock: 6:30 a.m. Maggie's breakfast shift didn't start until 8:00, but there she was, standing in the doorway, bawling her eyes out. I jumped to my feet, realizing that I wasn't wearing a shirt but thankful that I slept in shorts.

"Maggie?" I asked. "Maggie, what's wrong?"

Grandpa excused himself into his bedroom and closed the door behind him.

"What's wrong?" I asked again. I wrapped my arm around her shoulders, but she shooed me away, something she had never done before.

"I did a terrible thing," she cried. "And I'm so sorry." She wiped her tears away with the back of her hand. Her light skin was blotchy, like she had been crying all night.

"Sit down," I told her, gesturing to Grandpa's couch.

She nodded and sat down beside me, sobbing uncontrollably. "I… the picture… Grayson…" Her voice trailed off.

"Maggie," I started. "Maggie, you aren't making any sense." She nodded and made eye contact with me, and I could tell she wanted to calm down, but her emotions were taking over. "Here," I whispered. I lay down on the couch and pulled the covers over us, the closest we had ever been. She curled into me, so naturally, and collapsed, sobbing more. I held her for what felt like hours, wondering what she could have done with our picture that was so terrible.

"Maggie?" I whispered. "Whatever it is, it will be okay."

She sat up and shook her head. "It won't!" she cried. "West, the people that I got caught up with… the guy, Grayson, who said he was in a gang? It's bigger than I thought. He isn't who he said he was… It's bad, West. Really bad."

"Grayson?" I asked, confused. "Is he the guy that got you to trespass?"

She nodded her head. "Except… except he isn't really who he said he was. He isn't even…" she sobbed harder before catching her breath. "He isn't even my *age!*"

Her body shook and trembled, and although I was confused as all hell, all I could do was hold her tighter. "Then who was he?" I asked calmly. "What does this have to do with our picture?"

She pulled back and studied me. "I'm *so* sorry," she whispered again. "I posted our picture... from the other night. I posted it on my Myspace and my Facebook. And after I did, Grayson showed up at my house. I snuck out to see him... uh... I'm such an idiot, West. I shouldn't have trusted him. He asked me all kinds of questions... about where you are from..."

"Where *I'm* from?" I asked, suddenly confused. "Why would your friend want to know where I'm from?"

"Because!" she shouted. "Because he isn't who he said he is. He isn't a kid from a prep school. He's with the *paparazzi*."

I stiffened my shoulders and jumped up, confused. "What would the paparazzi want to do with you? With our picture?"

Maggie clenched her fists and let out a longer than expected wail. Grandpa stormed into the room, eyes wide, mouth gaping. "Because," she cried, reaching for her cell phone. "Your mother, she's—"

"What is the meaning of this?" Grandpa demanded.

"Let me see that," I said, taking the phone from Maggie's trembling hand.

"Your mother," Maggie repeated. "According to this, she's Silvia Flores. And I just helped a member of the paparazzi get a ton of money. Because... West... it's all over the news."

It had been days since Maggie approached me with her confession, and I hadn't been able to budge from the balcony of Grandpa's apartment. Under open sky with ocean air on my face was the only place I had wanted to be... alone.

I had been trying to find out about my mother for my entire life. How cruel was it that I'd found out this way? Even more surreal was the fact that I never stopped to notice the resemblance between me and Silvia Flores. Although I would never admit it, I had seen every episode of *Carolina Sands*. And I never once put the pieces together? A part of me felt sorry for Maggie. She fell straight into a trap. Apparently, reporters were offering a large sum of money to anyone that had evidence confirming a rumor that Silvia gave up a baby boy back in 1993. They tracked Maggie down on social media and found that she was a fan of the show on Facebook. They also made the connection to WVC through Gary Thatcher, her father. Apparently, they had a lead on Dad and me for years, but the photograph of me and Maggie on her social media pages, along with Grayson and his emotional manipulation drawing out Maggie's confession, had sealed the deal.

"Westly," Grandpa stammered. "Westly, I think it's time you come back inside."

I ignored him like I had done for the past forty-eight hours. "I'm fine," I barked. "I'm good out here."

Grandpa sat down next to me in his lounge chair and sighed. "Westly... I think it's time we talk about your mother."

"What about her?" I asked bitterly. "I've been trying to find out something, anything, for my entire life, and *now* you want to talk about her?"

"It's not that black and white." He sighed. "Your mother and father, they loved each other very much."

I crossed my arms over my head and sighed. I had waited seventeen years for this moment. And now, under the night sky of Wells, Maine, I wasn't sure I wanted to hear it. But either way, I let him carry on. "How did they meet?"

"They met in college," he started. "They dated for a while but broke up when your mother, Silvia, dropped out. She wanted to be an actress. It was a bad breakup, if I remember correctly. Your father was heartbroken."

I nodded my head. "So if they broke up, how did they end up having me?"

"Fair question," he agreed. "They broke up because your mother wanted to move out to LA and become an actress. They both moved on, but they ran into each other at a wedding of a mutual friend. One thing led to another, and…"

"And *bam*, they made me," I finished for him.

"Yes." He sighed. "They made you. And for the record, I'm glad they did."

I rubbed my hands through my hair and tried my best to ignore the painfully solemn expression spread across Grandpa's face. "So what happened? She just didn't want me?"

"Well, by the time your mother was pregnant with you, she had already filmed her first Oscar-nominated movie," he explained, as if this had anything to do with what I wanted to know. "So she didn't want to… she didn't want…"

"She didn't want me."

Grandpa sighed again. "It was complicated. She was very career driven, your mother. Your father asked her to at least carry you full term. They were planning on putting you up for adoption. They kept her out of the public eye long enough to deliver you… They had a family ready to adopt you, Westly."

I shook my head, realizing that this was more information than I wanted, but even still, I needed to hear it. "So what happened?"

"I begged your father to reconsider. I encouraged him… I told him to keep you."

My eyes grew wide, and an unwanted tear ran down my cheek. "You did?"

"I did. I promised that I would help him raise you. There were lawyers… agents… and we signed lots of papers. We promised that you would never be traced back to your mother again."

I sat, stunned, in the darkness. "My mother didn't want me," I repeated back to him.

"She wanted you," he affirmed. "But she wanted her career more."

"I think I've heard enough, Grandpa."

"I'm sure you have, Westly." Unsurprisingly, he sighed yet again. "But you've waited a long time to hear this, so I think you should know the truth. Your father and I, we wanted to name you Arthur, like us. But your mother insisted on Westly. She loved it out in Arizona—she loved it out west."

"And why do I need to hear this?" I snapped.

"Because, Westly. The day she named you, she held you in her arms. She kissed you on your tiny forehead, cried tears the size of golf balls, and told you she loved you. And I think it's important, after all these years, that you know how much your mother loved you, even if you only had that one moment together."

* * *

IT HAD BEEN a week since the press release about my mother, and because of the attention and publicity the story was receiving, I felt it best to stay locked away in Grandpa's apartment. I wasn't sure how long it had been since I had peeled myself from the couch. Could have been days or could have been hours. Grandpa was downstairs, playing cards, when Maggie showed up. She had knocked before entering, and I had cursed under my breath that I should have locked the door. She entered, wearing her tan shorts and black polo, a look of worry spread across her face. "I'm sorry to bother you," she stammered. "Can I come in?"

I nodded and cleared a spot for her on the couch. "I

wanted to say how sorry I am, West. I shouldn't have told Grayson anything about you."

I tightened my jaw, my hands automatically forming fists by my sides. "That's right," I said more sternly than I had meant to.

"It's just that… I didn't have a lot of friends before I met Grayson. I didn't have a lot of friends before I met you. And… I really care about you, West."

Suddenly, hearing my name out loud made my stomach turn. *West…* because my mother liked it out there? I suddenly wanted, needed, to change my name. "I really don't want to talk about it, Maggie."

"I know. And you have every reason to say that."

"That night," I started. "The night you were supposed to meet me… you were with him?"

She looked down at the floor and nodded. "Yes. He showed up at my door and told me that we needed to go for a walk. He wanted to explain what happened the night I got caught trespassing. I *had* to go… I had to know what happened that night."

"But instead of talking about the initiation, you told him all about *me.*"

"Yes," she said, choking on her words. "I don't know why I kept thinking I could trust him, West. He said *all* the right things. He told me… he told me he loved me. And then he talked about the picture I posted and wanted to know who you were. He made it seem like he was angry with me for seeing someone else." She placed her hands over her face and sobbed harder.

I stared straight ahead, not able to look her in the eyes. "Did you kiss him that night?" I closed my eyes and remembered how concerned I had been for her because I hadn't seen her all day. Thoughts flew through my mind at a million miles per hour, things I was going to say to her that night. *I* was going to tell Maggie how much I cared about her.

"Grayson?"

"Grayson."

She shrugged and started to cry again. "Yes. I don't know why, but yes."

I took a deep breath, determined to keep my emotions in check. "What did you tell him?"

"I'm such an idiot," she said, scolding herself. "He asked how I met you, and I told him that you stay with Grandpa at WVC. I told him that you travel each summer from Scottsdale, Arizona. I told him that you... that you didn't know your mother." She sobbed. "I'm so sorry. I hope that we can still be friends."

With that, something inside of me snapped. *Friends?* If she only knew how much I liked her. I had never opened myself up to anyone like I had opened up to Maggie. I had never pictured myself even being with anyone prior to meeting her. And look where it got me. Suddenly, the blood began rushing through my veins, and I needed to hit something, anything. I found a couch cushion and ripped it off the couch and slammed it to the ground. An unfamiliar animal-like roar came pouring out of me, and it was all I could do to stop myself from pounding my fist against the wall.

"West!" Maggie cried out. The look of terror spread across her face spoke volumes, and for a moment, I was forced to drop to the floor with my face between my knees.

"I... I really cared about you, Maggie," I shouted between breaths.

"I really cared about you, too, West." She placed a trembling hand on my shoulder, and I shook it off. "Can you give me another chance?" she pleaded again. "I know it's a lot to ask of you, considering I went and screwed everything up."

"We can be friends," I sighed. "But, Maggie, I will *never* be able to trust you again… not like *that.*"

She jumped back, eyes wide. "What do you mean?"

"I mean, we can be friends. But we can *never* be more than that."

"You don't mean that," she demanded between sobs. "I said I was sorry. Maybe if we just give it time—"

"*Never,*" I repeated. "Never in a billion years can we ever be more than friends. I can forgive you for this, Maggie, but it can't be more than friendship. Promise me. Promise me we will only be friends. If you can't promise that, then—"

Maggie dropped down on the ground next to me and wrapped her arm over my shoulder. She smelled like the dining hall and fruity shampoo, and for a moment, I considered taking back my words. But my heart had just exploded to smithereens, and my world was crumbling around me. I didn't believe in love anymore. I didn't believe in happily ever after, and for a moment, I wondered if I ever truly had.

"Never," she promised. She spoke slowly and steadily. "Never in a billion years will we ever be more than friends, West. Just please… promise you will always be my friend."

"I promise."

CHAPTER TEN- NOW

MAGGIE

ONE MONTH BEFORE THE BIG DAY

There were times at night when I couldn't fall asleep, and the only way I was able to close my eyes and drift away was to remember those moments; the short time that West and I had together before I sold his soul to the devil were some of the best times of my life. Of course, we continued to make memories together after the incident, but it was just different. We held each other to the promise we made that night in Art's condo. There was a piece of me that truly believed that we were able to stay close amidst the years that followed strictly because we promised to be nothing more.

It had taken a while for West's life to get back to normal after Silvia's story leaked and the world learned that the practically perfect Silvia Flores gave up her baby in the late nineties and covered it up with secrets and lies. Thankfully, Silvia wasn't as well known on the West Coast as she was on the East Coast, so when he did retreat to Arizona that summer, things were able to quiet down for him. His mother, however, took it upon herself to reach out to him once the story broke. He refused visits with her and turned down reporters and media day after day for what seemed like years.

I'm not sure I ever got over the pain and heartbreak that came with the betrayal of Grayson Astor and everything that followed his manipulative actions and untruthful alibi. When my father found out the reality of what happened with Grayson, I was scared to death that he was going to rip him apart with his bare hands. He didn't have to rip him apart, however, because fake Grayson dug his own grave. He was a nineteen-year-old reporter and member of the paparazzi, and he failed to realize that by having "relations" with me, as the police officer called it, he was breaking the law. Fake Grayson got his payday, but he also served some jail time.

"It's crazy being back here," West says, snatching me out of my thoughts.

"It must be. I can't imagine being away from the ocean for so long."

It has been years since West and I have walked on the beach together. We stroll, side by side, under the moonlight. The sounds of laughter and music from the piano bar seem so close but at the same time, so far away. I study the full moon behind the outline of the clouds against the dark sky and, by habit, begin counting the stars.

West stops in his tracks, and I know he is about to make serious conversation because that is what West does. "Maggie, we need to talk."

"I know," I say calmly.

"You know?"

"Well," I start. "I know you have something to tell me. I don't know exactly what you need to tell me. But I'm assuming I'm not going to like it."

West chuckled. "Oh yeah? How do you know?"

I put my hands in the pockets of my jean skirt and kick the water away with my toes. "Because, West Young... I'm your best friend. That's why. So, out with it. Why did you fly across the country today?"

I nudge him playfully with my elbow, and he surprises me by lightly grasping my shoulders in his hands. They feel warm and strong against my bare skin. "Maggie," he starts, then he stops for a moment before speaking again. "Maggie... I'm getting married."

There are times when things feel out of my control and I want to scream, cry, swear, and kick something. This is surely one of those times. But I can't freak out, and I can't lose control, because I love this man... and I want what's best for him more than anything else in the world, even more than I want what's best for me. "Okay," I say, chewing on my bottom lip. "It's Natalia, isn't it?" I ask like I am confirming his terminal diagnosis.

West takes my hands in his and nods. "Yes, Maggie. I'm marrying Natalia."

I *despise* Natalia Bartolome. Not only because she swept West off his feet during a bachelor party that he attended in Los Angeles one year ago, and *really* not just because she models swimsuits for a living, but because I have a theory. That Natalia is using West as a way of making it big in Hollywood... After all, he *is* the son of Silvia Flores. But I'm not sure what hurts more, the fact that she could be using this marriage as a way to bust her way into West's family tree or that she gets to be with him and I *don't*—and now I never will.

"Maggie? Are you okay? You're turning colors."

I release his hands from mind and shake my head from side to side. "Me? Of course. Wow! Congratulations, West. This is... wow... this is great news."

West rubs my arms like he is trying to warm them up... or like a football coach encouraging his player before he heads in for the next play. "Yeah," he says. "It's really great news."

I turn and continue walking, hopeful that he can't see the tears that are welling up in the corners of my glassy eyes. Of course he is getting married. He has been with Natalia for a year, which in West's world is a lifetime. I might not be Natalia's biggest fan, but I can step up to the plate and be happy for him... if I must. The truth is, if the right guy came along, I, too, would probably snag him up. I dated Seth off and on for a while, and that didn't work out because... well, he isn't West. "So, when's the wedding?" I ask, at this point settling with small talk.

"That's the thing," he said, stopping me again. "It's in a month, Maggie."

"A month?" I shriek. "You're getting married in a month?" I begin pacing around him like a lunatic. "You are getting *married* in a *month*."

"Yeah. One month from today."

I stop in my tracks and point an accusatory finger at West. "You knocked her up?" I yell louder than intended. "Seriously, West, didn't your father ever talk to you about birth control?"

West laughs and shakes his head. "I didn't get her pregnant, Maggie. It's what we want. We don't want a long, drawn-out engagement. We just want to get married."

We. I try not to throw up in my mouth. "That's... different," I mumble.

West pulls me close and squeezes me. My head rests on his chest, and I close my eyes. It's the closest I've ever been to him, and I confirm in that moment, it is one of my favorite places to be. "I'm happy for you. Just surprised—that's all."

"There's more."

"Honestly, West." I sigh. "I don't know how much more of this I can take."

He laughs, and I realize that he thinks I'm kidding. "I know it's short notice, but will you be my best man?"

I let out a strange, frustrated whimper. "Yes," I whisper into his shirt. "I'll be your best man." Because I want absolutely nothing to do with Natalia Bartolome or this engagement, but it is better than nothing. *Keep your friends close and your enemies closer*—an expression Art Young taught me long ago. And in this moment, in the comfort of West's embrace, I intend on doing just that.

PART TWO

CHAPTER ELEVEN- NOW

MAGGIE

ONE WEEK BEFORE THE BIG DAY

*T*he Nubble Lighthouse rests on an island of emerald green and seems to tower over me and Finley. My chocolate-brown Labrador retriever sniffs his way around the area while I study the historical landmark and wonder what my life would have been like if I never met Grayson Astor in the first place. On one hand, I would have avoided being in trouble with the law, which is always a plus. But on the flip side, I might not have ever met West or Art. Or maybe I would have, and maybe, if it were under different circumstances, I wouldn't have completely blown it with West, and we could be more than friends.

The years seemed to have gone by in the blink of an eye since that summer of 2010. West flew back to Arizona, and I grew closer to Art Young. He took me under his wing, insisting that I was better than the girl who was serving community service for a trespassing crime. Art had an outlook on life that I had never been subjected to before. When West left for Arizona, still angry with me, it was Art who helped me pick up the pieces.

"That last wave knocked you down good!" he exclaimed.

"Now you need to get back up and get ready for the next one. One wave at a time, Maggie. One wave at a time."

But what about the fact that I can't choose my waves? Sure, I can take life one wave at a time, but what if the waves I am being dealt are just plain shitty? I received the email from the interview team from WVC only two days after meeting with them. *Thank you for interviewing for the administrative position*, they wrote. *We regret to inform you that we have chosen to move forward with another candidate.*

Then there is also the fact that in just one short week, I will be packing up and heading to Scottsdale, Arizona, for my best friend's wedding... as his best man. Which sounds a lot like a movie I've seen before, or maybe a nightmare, I'm not sure which. It wouldn't be so bad if I wasn't convinced that *I* should be marrying Westly Young, not Natalia Bartolome.

"Come on, Finley," I called. "Mommy needs to get to work."

* * *

"Good morning, Miss Thatcher." Seth is at the retirement center door.

I roll my eyes. "Seth, this is starting to feel a little like Groundhog Day. You don't have to call me Miss Thatcher."

I adjust my tote on my shoulder and balance my coffee cup while fixing my hair. "But thank you."

"You're welcome, Miss Thatcher," he says with a wink.

I nod and smile at him, taking my last sip of coffee before tossing it in a nearby trash can. "Have a good day, Seth," I call over my shoulder.

I hurry down the hallway to my office, eager to put the finishing touches on a few last-minute projects before my departure to Arizona next week.

The buzzing of my cell phone snaps me out of the list of things to do that is running through my mind. Kendra's name lights up the screen. "No!" I shriek out loud. "Kendra," I say into my cell as I open the door to my office. "Tell me you have good news."

"I wish I did." She sighs. "It's Art again."

"I'm covering for a tour in an hour. I don't have much time. Where is he now?"

"On the beach. Where else?"

FORTY-FIVE MINUTES LATER, I have retrieved Art Young from the ocean. At first, he didn't budge, but when I started to talk his ear off about his grandson's upcoming marriage being the biggest mistake of his life, he moved swiftly from the water back onto the beach. I also promised him that he could help me with my tour. I don't typically give tours, but my father asked me to fill in for his director of client services, and since I am not getting a promotion anytime soon, I may as well kiss up when I can.

I make my way to the front door with Art Young straggling close behind. Seth is in his usual spot, looking better than ever, and again, I find myself wondering why it is that we broke up. He runs his hand through his dirty-blond hair. "Nice to see you again, Miss Thatcher. Giving a tour today?"

"That's right," I say, glancing toward Art, who has changed into a clean pair of khakis and a new Hawaiian shirt. I brush the beach sand off my legs and smile. "And Arthur here is going to be my assistant."

"Very nice," he says, smiling. "I'm sure Arthur will make a great assistant."

I check the time on my phone and grunt in aggravation. I

despise giving tours because they never seem to start when they are supposed to, and I have a ton of work to do.

"I'm going to grab a coffee," Art explains. "Don't start without me."

"I won't."

Art struts away toward the coffee shop, leaving Seth and me waiting awkwardly at the front door.

I glance down at my cell and begin scrolling through my text messages in an effort to make this moment of silence with him a bit less painful. Jordan, my sister, was the last person to text me.

Jordan: *How's it going? Are you ready for the wedding?*

Maggie: *I don't think I will ever be ready for this wedding.*

Jordan: *Do you have to go? You could always come visit us instead.*

I think about this for a moment. Jordan lives in southern Florida with her husband and her three-year-old daughter, Hayden. The thought of spending some quality time with them suddenly seems fabulous in comparison to flying across the country to watch West marry Natalia.

Maggie: *I'll think about it. I already have a plane ticket to Phoenix, and I AM the best man (insert eye roll emoji)*

"So," Seth leans down and whispers in my ear while continuing to stare straight ahead at the door like an under-cover police officer trying to keep his cover, "I was thinking."

"What were you thinking now, Seth?" I ask, annoyed that I am standing here making small talk with Seth Jenson when I have a million other things to do before my trip. Between my usual daily tasks and Art's sudden need for quality time, I am quickly running out of patience.

My eyes return to my cell phone's screen, and I briskly tap the keys in an effort to return more messages.

West: *Just emailed you hotel information... best bar around right in the lobby... they make prickly pear martinis.*

Maggie: *What the HELL is a prickly pear?*

West: *I guess you will just have to wait and see.*

I swipe out of my texts and open my internet browser then type *prickly pear* into the search bar. "It's the flowering part of the cactus," I mutter under my breath.

"Huh?" Seth asks.

"Nothing."

"Like I was saying... you and me," he whispers, his voice doing that deep and sexy thing that it sometimes does.

"You and me what?" I ask, suddenly taken off guard. My cheeks brighten, and my knees grow weak.

"Tonight. You and me. Your place. I *miss* you, Maggie."

I turn away from Seth, knowing in my heart that the possibility of a relationship with him has sailed... but also eager to remove the idea of West and Natalia and their upcoming wedding from my mind. I am torn between what I know is right and the possibility of repairing the broken piece of me. I'm not sure what is worse, a broken heart or an exposed open wound that will never quite heal. I decide that if I can't fix the situation, I may as well put a Band-Aid on it. "Fine," I whisper. "After work."

"Six o'clock?"

"Seven. I have to pick up Finley from doggy daycare."

"Seven is perfect, Miss Thatcher."

The door budges open, and Seth almost misses his chance to do his job, but he is quick. "Welcome to Wells Valley Cove," he states with confidence as an elderly woman and her family enter the facility.

"Hi," I say in my happiest, most professional tour voice possible. "I'm Maggie. Are you Kathryn Roy? Here for a tour?"

She nods her head slowly and nervously looks around, hugging her handbag close to her chest. "Yes," she says. "My granddaughter would like me to tour this facility. I've told her time and time again that it is quite all right for an eighty-year-old single woman to live on her own, but she insists that I need to socialize and be around other people my age. Isn't that right, Grace?"

I smile and nod at Grace and welcome her family into the building. "We are glad to have you," I start. "This is our main common area, accessible to residents in independent and assisted living. We have a gift shop, café, dining hall, and an activities facility."

"My great grandfather is a nursing home patient here," Grace explains. "I am familiar with the nursing home wing, but this is our first time exploring the other amenities that you have to offer. He is approaching one hundred one years old this January." The young woman is beaming.

I smile, thinking of some of my favorite one-hundred-year-old friends and how close we have grown over the years. "We have a few assisted living and nursing home patients that are over one hundred."

"Can I spend time on the beach?" Kathryn asks. "That is the only reason I agreed to this in the first place."

"Nana loves the beach," Grace offers. "She can't get enough of it."

"Our private beach is stunning—"

"I told you not to start without me!" Art scolds from behind me. I turn to see him approaching, coffee cup in hand, sipping as he walks. "I'm the best tour guide you can get around here. I've been living here for—" Art stops in his tracks and, in one instant, has turned white as a ghost.

"Hi Art," I sing. "I was just about to introduce you to Kathryn Roy."

"Katie?" his voice quivers, and his hands tremble. I quickly remove the coffee from Art's grasp so it doesn't end up splattering all over the ground. "Kathryn Roy... is that really you? I'll be damned!"

CHAPTER TWELVE- 1959

ART

I guzzled my coffee at the small table in the kitchen of the Anderson Cottage, first floor. My small living space might not have seemed like much to most people, but to me, it meant one thing—freedom. It was the summer of my eighteenth birthday, and although I was still only seventeen years old, my parents had caved and given me the okay to rent on the first floor, by myself, if I saved up enough money to be officially out on my own by the end of the summer. The truth was that I would have agreed to anything they wanted in order to spend the summer on Long Sands Beach. I had already been lifeguarding on Long Sands for two years at that point, and the beach was the only place I ever wanted to be.

Everything had been going smoothly, at first. That was, until my girlfriend, Gloria, broke up with me. We had been parked in my blue 1955 Ford Thunderbird overlooking the Nubble Lighthouse when it happened. "We have the *whole* summer ahead of us, Art," she had tried to explain between sobs. "It just doesn't make sense that we would want to be tied down right now. We have our whole lives ahead of us."

"Aw, shucks, Gloria," I had said. "You're really doing this now? At the start of the summer? I just got the first floor of the Anderson Cottage all to myself."

"That's exactly why we are breaking this off now, Arthur Young. You're moving too fast."

"Don't be a wet rag, Gloria. We could have a good time, you and me." I grabbed the back of her head and pulled her in for a kiss, like I had done a dozen times before.

"A wet rag? I'll give you a wet rag." With that, she pulled her waist-length black hair off her neck, grabbed her beach bag, and exited the car, slamming the door behind her. "Have a nice life, Arthur Young," she snapped. "We are through, you and me."

Gloria and I had been going steady for the last two years of high school. To see her walk away like that, with no good reason, was a tough pill to swallow. But I decided that I was going to make the best of the summer no matter what. The Anderson Cottage on Long Sands Beach would be my refuge.

I stretched my arms overhead and sighed. Having a place of my own would still be a blast, even without Gloria. Besides, having the cottage to myself had its positives, and I had already grown to appreciate the calming and dreamy vibe that it somehow manifested all on its own. I glanced around the kitchen. It was a tad on the small side but, nevertheless, nicely decorated. The geometric-style wallpaper of orange, teal, and yellow covered the walls of the minuscule kitchen. An antique brown couch was positioned to face a red-brick fireplace adjacent to the tiny kitchen table, which sat atop a shaggy yellow carpet.

"Hello in there," a voice called from the doorway. "Anybody home?"

"Yes," I called back in the deepest, most mature-sounding voice I could muster. "Come in."

"You must be Arthur!" the man exclaimed. "I'm Joey

Chase. Your mother has told me a lot about you." My mother had mentioned that I would be meeting him at the cottage that afternoon and had made it a point to remind me to use my best manners.

"Yes," I started. "Arthur—Art Young."

I extended my hand for a handshake, and he did the same. He appeared to be in his early thirties. He had a friendly smile, and he ran his hand through his unkempt brown hair as he spoke. "Nice to meet you, Art. I hope you enjoy your time here at the Anderson Cottage. This is a very special place."

"I can sense that already," I agreed. "Thank you for having me. Do you live here?"

"I live in Boston, but I am the keeper of the property, and it turns out I will be vacationing upstairs, on the second floor, for the summer with my wife, Gwendoline, and our daughter, Elizabeth. She just turned fourteen this past October and begged us to spend the summer here. Should be quite the vacation; you should come up for dinner sometime."

I took a sip of coffee and smiled my most polite smile, as the last thing I wanted to do this summer was have family dinner; I had my own family for that. But I remembered my manners, knowing that turning down such a gracious offer would be rude and secretly afraid of what my mother would say. "Thank you. I'm lifeguarding on Long Sands, and that's where I plan on spending most of my time, lifeguarding and surfing... but I would love to take you up on your offer at some point."

"Very nice, son. We are here if you need us. Gwendoline makes a delicious pot roast dinner, a recipe that has been in our family for years. We also invited some friends from Boston... the Roy family. They will be staying up on the third floor and might be popping in to say hello."

"Thanks, Joey, I appreciate it. Thank you for letting me rent the space. It was nice to meet you."

"Nice to meet you, too, Art. You have yourself a great summer."

Joey stopped and glanced around the room. I wasn't positive, but I was pretty sure he was staring at the old plaid couch, smiling like he was either recalling a special memory or knew a juicy secret.

CHAPTER THIRTEEN- 1959

KATIE

*I*t was going to be the best summer of my life. Not only because I was turning sixteen years old that July, but for the first time in my entire life, I finally had a taste of the one thing I had always wanted—freedom.

The Anderson Cottage was all I could have hoped for and more. The tall gray house seemed to tower over all the others on Long Sands Beach. The three-story gray cottage was special for many reasons, but my favorite part about it was that each floor had a fenced-in balcony that overlooked Long Sands.

"I want to live here forever," I told my mother as I unpacked my suitcase. The third floor of the Anderson Cottage was beyond perfect. The quaint kitchen was adjacent to a living room with a porch and a table that was perfect for having coffee or tea. My bedroom was my favorite. Although it didn't overlook the ocean, it had the most precious little rocking chair and the perfect twin-sized bed. I sat for a moment in the white chair and wrapped the navy-blue blanket around my shoulders. "I want to live here forever," I repeated, this time to myself.

I knew Elizabeth Chase from our neighborhood in South Boston. We went to school together, but she was one grade below me. We met working on the school newspaper and both aspired to be writers. Although she was a tad bit younger than me, it often felt as though we were sisters. We became close, Elizabeth and I, and naturally, so did our parents. Her mother and father, Gwendoline and Joey, were some of my favorite people. So when her family invited me to stay with them at the Anderson Cottage, I was over-the-moon excited. Elizabeth had shared with me the story of how her parents met back in the forties about ninety-nine times, and if I could hear it again for the hundredth time, it would still not get old.

Elizabeth's mother, Gwendoline, had been dating Gerry Anderson, who was living on the first floor of the Anderson Cottage back during the Second World War. Joey had been living on the third floor and was best friends with Gerry. They all used to go dancing together, Gerry, Joey, and Gwendoline. Gerry didn't like to dance to fast songs, so he charged Joey in beers to dance with Gwendoline (if you ask me, that was his first big mistake).

Soon after the attack on Pearl Harbor, Gerry enlisted in the United States Navy and, after marrying Gwendoline at the Union Bluff Hotel, departed overseas to fight for our country. He also entrusted Joey with Gwendoline, asking him to take care of her while he was gone. Well, Joey did more than *just* take care of Gwendoline. I would share the details, but quite frankly, I find it a tad on the embarrassing side. Long story short, Gerry stopped writing, and it was assumed something terrible had happened to him. Joey and Gwendoline grew close—a little too close—and Gwendoline ended up pregnant (oh, the scandal!) and tried to pretend the baby (Elizabeth) was Gerry's. But get this: the whole time Gwendoline and Joey were messing around, Gerry was having an affair with his nurse overseas, whom he ended up marrying years later. I couldn't write that stuff if I tried.

I did love that story for many reasons. First, because it was a story about love and sacrifice, but also because it served as a reminder to me that there was a person out there for everyone—that one soulmate. And even if the road got bumpy at first, life sometimes just had a way of working things out. I also found their love story intriguing because of the way that Elizabeth's parents looked at one another, and I secretly hoped and prayed that somehow, someday, I would find my own Joey Chase.

* * *

"Are you ready to go to the beach, Katie?" Elizabeth called from the doorway. Her shoulder-length ginger hair was pulled back in a ponytail, and her short bangs fell just above her eyes. It was a hairstyle she had copied from me, but I didn't mind.

"Yes," I called back. "Just grabbing my things."

"I'll wait in the kitchen."

"I'll be there in five minutes." I studied my reflection in my bedroom mirror. I was short for my age, and I despised that more than anything. I adjusted the shorts of my one-piece swimsuit and checked once again that the back was tied tightly. I had wanted, more than anything, to be able to wear a bikini to the beach that summer, but my father had not been on board with the idea.

"Over my dead body," he had insisted, "will any daughter of mine be caught on the beach naked."

I ran my fingers through my chestnut-colored bangs and adjusted my ponytail. I found my favorite red lipstick and applied it carefully, appreciating the life it brought to my features and the years it seemed to add on to my appearance... Why, I could have passed for at least seventeen years old. I reached for my beach bag, closed the door behind me, and headed for the kitchen, where Elizabeth was speaking with my father.

"You two girls have fun," he was saying. "But make sure you stay where the lifeguards can see you... and don't go out past here," he instructed, gesturing to his waist.

I rolled my eyes. "Daddy, I'm about to be sixteen. You really need to—"

He held his hand up as if to say, *Enough*, and kissed me on the forehead. "You will always be my little girl, Kathryn. Have fun and be back by dark."

THE WATER WAS COLDER than I had expected. Elizabeth explained that the ocean in Maine wasn't the warmest but told me I would be used to it in no time. After a few minutes of wading in the water and floating over the larger-than-expected waves, I didn't mind anymore.

"Your dad," Elizabeth started. "He's still really nervous about the water?"

I thought for a moment and frowned. "He is," I agreed. "But I don't really blame him, you know?"

Elizabeth had been referring to the fact that my overly protective father had been uneasy about the water... and rightfully so. When I was shy of 4 months old, my sister, Betty, had passed away tragically. She had wandered away from my mother, who was visiting a friend at a town pool. My mother had been feeding me a bottle and talking with her friend. Even though there were lifeguards on duty, Betty, just two years old at the time, fell into the pool, and by the time she was noticed, it had been too late.

"I don't think they will ever get over it. Honestly, I don't think I should expect them to." I ducked under an incoming wave and allowed the coolness of the water to soothe the ache I carried around with me for my sister. I didn't remember her at all, which made grieving her that much harder. But the weight of the accident took a toll on my parents. Although they were both in their early thirties, they were often mistaken as much older. "Anyways," I said. "Maybe we could talk about something else?"

"Understood," Elizabeth said, then with a giggle, "Careful. We are drifting away from the lifeguard stand."

I turned, and my gaze landed on a male lifeguard, and for a moment, my heart stopped beating. I was physically unable to take my eyes off him. It was like he was plucked out of the movies and dropped right smack on this beach for my viewing pleasure. He appeared sun-kissed, with a tan I would have died for and natural blond streaks in his light-brown hair. He wore only a pair of red lifeguard shorts, leaving his well-defined physique exposed with no room for the imagination. "Who. Is. That?" I asked.

"I don't know, but I think you're drooling, Katie."

I splashed Elizabeth playfully and giggled. "With good reason." I retied the top of my suit, as it had started to come loose, just as the lifeguard hopped down from his chair and blew his whistle at a surfer who appeared to be too far out in the water.

"Too far," he hollered between whistles. He kicked through the water, and within no time, he stood within six feet of us, blowing his whistle until the surfer acknowledged him and made his way closer to shore.

"Thank you!" he hollered, shaking his head from side to side. "Is he cruisin' for a bruisin', or what?" he asked. I couldn't tell if he was talking to himself or to us, but in that moment, I didn't care. I needed to talk to this hot stud muffin, and nothing was going to stop me.

"The nerve of him!" I yelled, more loudly than I meant to.

He took his eyes off the water and looked toward Elizabeth and me. Elizabeth, who was completely and utterly shocked by my boldness, couldn't control her laughter and ducked into an incoming wave.

"Yeah," he agreed. "Some nerve."

I stood up as straight as I could and pushed my chest forward in my best attempt to appear older, as I could tell this gentleman had at least a year on me. "Some people just don't respect authority," I said with a sigh.

He chuckled. "No, I suppose they don't."

Then he smiled at me, and my entire world was turned upside down. He was so handsome that he couldn't have been real. I must have been dreaming.

"Nice day for a swim," I said nervously.

"It's always a nice day for a swim if you ask me. Do I know you from somewhere?"

"Probably not. I'm from Boston. I just got here."

"Boston, huh? Are you staying over at the Anderson pad?"

Elizabeth splashed around me like a child, and I silently begged her to stop. "Yes, she is!" she hollered between splashes. "Anderson Cottage, third floor!"

I clenched my teeth, and for a moment, I was thankful for her honesty, but the truth was I didn't know him, although I *really* wanted to get to know him.

He replied, "I'm staying there for the summer... first floor."

I attempted to hide my excitement but failed miserably. I tried to keep my voice cool and calm. "That's great," I said, but on the inside, I was screaming.

"My name's Arthur. My friends call me Art."

"Hi, Art. It's a pleasure to meet you."

"I'm going to get back to work. See you around, I hope."

CHAPTER FOURTEEN- NOW

MAGGIE

ONE WEEK BEFORE THE BIG DAY

*I*t takes me roughly half an hour to commute from work to the Seaberry, my tiny cottage off Long Sands Beach, and then an extra ten minutes to swing and retrieve Finley from doggy daycare. The Seaberry is typically a rental, but I struck a deal with Mr. Elrod, an assisted living resident at WVC, who owns the property. Once Mrs. Elrod passed away in 2015, he didn't have the time or the energy to worry about vacation rentals. I, for one, was over-the-moon excited, as the Seaberry was my little piece of paradise, and I didn't want to give it up.

Normally, I would utilize my short commute home to decompress and unwind but not tonight, because tonight, I was stuck at work dealing with Art. Art, for whatever reason, lost his mind when faced with Kathryn Roy—so much so Seth and I were ready to get him medical attention. He refused, in typical Art fashion, and instead locked himself in his apartment, also refusing to come out for the rest of the day.

"What did you do to that poor man, Nana?" Grace had

asked her grandmother. "Who is he? I've never met him before."

"We were friends… once," Kathryn explained. There was no denying that she was shaken by Art's presence.

Thankfully, our tour went flawlessly after that. But the remainder of my day was consumed with worry over Art and his sudden need to lock himself away. And now I will have just about ten minutes to clean up around the Seaberry and change out of my work clothes, because tonight, I have sold my soul to the devil: Seth Jenson.

* * *

I ZIP up my skinny jeans and switch into my favorite maroon-striped tank top just as the clock over my stove changes to seven on the dot. I zoom around the cottage in an effort to declutter the living room and hide any evidence of the fact that I am not the best housekeeper. Very rarely do I ever clean up my cottage, unless I am having company. And the truth is that these days, I don't have much company.

I frantically gather piles of dirty clothes and stuff them in random closets. I wipe down the rustic countertop that separates the kitchen from the living room, light my favorite candle, and sigh with relief. To most people, the Seaberry isn't anything spectacular, but to me, the maple woodwork of the walls and ceiling offer a coziness that I can never really put my finger on. I dash back into my tiny bedroom and quickly make my bed—something I never do, ever. Seth knocks on the door just as I finish dousing myself with my favorite body spray.

"Come in!" I call from the bathroom, suddenly more nervous than I expected. *It's Seth Jenson, Maggie,* I think to myself. *Get it together.*

Seth lets himself in like he has done frequently over the

years. The sound of him entering the Seaberry and kicking his shoes off at the door comforts me in a way I hadn't expected.

"I brought pizza! And beer!"

"Awesome!" I call back, quickly running a brush through my blond hair.

Seth is already opening two bottles of beer when I reenter the kitchen. "Good evening, Miss Thatcher," he says with a wink. He, too, has changed out of his work clothes. It has been a while since I have been with him outside of work. The familiarity of him leaning over my counter in his Under Armour sweatpants and favorite gray hoodie makes my insides tingle and my heart feel all sorts of confused.

"Good evening, Mr. Jenson," I reply more flirtatiously than I mean to. "Thanks for the pizza. I'm starving."

* * *

HALF AN HOUR LATER, Seth and I have crushed an entire large cheese pizza and a six-pack of Sam Summer. We are seated on the couch in the tiny living room of the Seaberry, Luke Bryan (our favorite country artist) serenading us from my Alexa.

Seth takes his last swig of beer and places his arm around my shoulder. "Remember when we saw him in concert?"

I smile, remembering the night that Seth surprised me with tickets to see Luke. "My hips still hurt from shaking." I laugh.

"You were a dancing machine!"

I punch him playfully. "He told me to shake it."

I lean my head on his shoulder and take in his familiar smell: Irish Spring soap and Aveda shampoo. I know this because more times than not, when I would occasionally stay at his place, I would use his toiletries. I close my eyes and do my best to ignore the racing of my heart, and I try even harder to forget how good the nights felt when we showered together, the gentle way he lathered his Aveda men's shampoo through my hair, the tender way he washed my back with his Irish Spring bar soap.

"Luke said, '*Country girl*, shake it for me.' Not '*Maggie Thatcher*, shake it for me.'" Seth is grinning at me, evidently proud of himself.

"Huh?" I ask, my mind *so* not on Luke Bryan anymore.

"The concert. You said—"

Seth's words are cut short because I reach up and grab his face, pulling it close to mine. Within seconds, I am straddling him on the sofa, our lips dancing together in harmony. I lift Seth's sweatshirt off him and toss it to the side then trace my hands under his T-shirt, first over his chest and then his back.

"Maggie," Seth whispers between kisses. "What are we doing?"

Trying to forget, I think as I run my hands through his thick blond hair and lean in for another kiss.

"Maggie?" he asks again.

I ignore him once more, fighting with all my might to forget the words that rolled so easily off West's tongue that night on the beach. *Natalia and I... we are getting married.*

I unzip my jeans, and although Seth continues verbally questioning my judgment, he helps me scoot them off and reaches under my shirt with ease. I kiss him again, harder this time, removing his T-shirt and then my own.

Seth takes my hand and leads me to my bedroom, a place he is no stranger to.

"You made your bed," he says, snickering. "First time for everything."

I nod and lie down on my bed, pulling him on top of me,

wrapping my legs around his waist and kissing his lips, his neck, and then his ear.

"Maggie," he moans.

I reach under his arms, spinning us and pinning him down on his back as I climb on top of him, my lips tracing over his defined pecs.

"What are we doing?" he asks between breaths.

"It's fine, West," I moan. "Just kiss me."

Seth's eyes pop open, and he shudders like he has been punched in the gut, and it doesn't take more than a second before I realize what I've done.

"West?" he asks, between breaths. "You just—"

I collapse my body lifelessly onto his torso and shove my face into my pillow and grunt. For a moment, the only thing I can hear is Seth's heart beating rapidly against my chest. "Slip of the tongue?" I offer meekly.

Seth rolls me off him and lies on his back, his chest rising and falling heavily. "You know it wasn't a slip of the tongue… again."

I rub my hands over my eyes and groan in frustration. "Can we pretend that didn't happen? Please? It was a mistake."

I roll onto my side and stare into his eyes, heartbroken because I have clearly caused him pain. Does he really think this is more than just a hookup? Isn't that all this was? Clearly, he must realize that what we had is over.

He runs his hands through my hair and kisses my cheek. "I *really* like you, Maggie. But this West guy… he really messed you up. When are you going to see that he just isn't worth it?"

"Seth—"

"One of these days, Maggie. Maybe you will see that you don't need him. Maybe you'll realize that what you need is me."

With that, he gathers his things and leaves me there, on my bed by myself, half naked, wondering what I need to do to get over West—the man I want to be with more than anyone else in this world—a man who doesn't want to be with me.

CHAPTER FIFTEEN- 1959

ART

I clutched the yellow surfboard against my side, eager to hit the waves after a long day of blowing my whistle at idiots who couldn't seem to understand where they were allowed to swim and where they were not. It had been a week since I moved into the Anderson Cottage, and this was the first time I would be able to get out on some decent-sized waves.

The sea welcomed me with open arms as it usually did. Growing up, if I ever had a hard day at school or if my parents were exceptionally harsh on me for one reason or another, I always found refuge in the comfort of the Atlantic. It didn't matter how big or small a problem was—the ocean made it better. It was the equivalent of air to my lungs.

I lay prone on my board and paddled out past the breaking waves. This was my favorite part of surfing. I could float, like a buoy, over each wave… or I could choose the one I wanted and just go for it. Either way, I was in control. And if the ride didn't work out, I would just patiently wait for another.

The perfect wave rose behind me, and I decided it would

be mine. I paddled through the thick ocean water until I felt the steady push of the wave under my board and jumped up, riding it to shore. When there was nothing left to ride, I hopped off the side, landing in the ankle-deep water with little effort.

"Hey there."

The sun was in my eyes, but I knew who it was before I could see her. Katie Roy, the girl who was living on the third floor with her mother and father. Katie Roy, the most beautiful girl I had ever laid eyes on.

"Hi, Katie." I nodded, turning back to the ocean, ready for my next ride.

"That was great!" she called out, following me into the water. I turned back and studied her, her red-and-black bathing suit stuck to her body in all the right ways. Her red lipstick drew attention to her more-than-kissable lips. But I had done some digging on her, and for a guy that was about to turn eighteen, she was just too young.

"Thanks. I'm heading back out."

"Okay," she called, clearly disappointed. "Do you think you could show me sometime?"

"Show you what?"

"How to surf. I want to learn how to surf," she stated firmly.

"Okay, Gidget," I chuckled. "Why don't you go splash in the waves with your friends in the shallow end?"

"Because," she stated firmly, arms crossed. "I want to surf."

"They have lessons down the street," I explained. "They will set you up with some baby waves and a nice long board. Those are perfect for ankle-biters like you."

I wasn't trying to be rude, but she simply wasn't old enough. And if I was going to spend the entire summer with her living on the third floor of the Anderson Cottage, I would need to lay down the law now. I trudged through the breaking surf and dropped down on my board once again, paddling out into the serenity and stillness of the open water, trying to get the image of Katie and her red lipstick out of my mind.

* * *

THE WATER WAS ROUGHER than normal, and it was probably due to the storm that would be coming through. I scanned the beach with my eyes as I had done hundreds of times before. Most of the beachgoers on Long Sands were families with young children, and there was no way I was going to let a little kid get dragged out under the larger-than-normal swells. I had blown my whistle three times in the last ten minutes and was eager for my shift to be over. Lifeguarding was great, but in this mess, it was kind of overwhelming.

Gloria had approached the lifeguard stand earlier that afternoon. I wasn't quite sure what her intentions were, but man, did she look good. She wore one of those high-waisted bikinis that all the girls were wearing. It was red and white polka-dotted, and for a moment, I was furious that she was flaunting herself around like that. I wouldn't call it jealous, as I missed her a little… but not a lot. I was just nervous for her, I suppose. Guys could be pigs, as I knew firsthand. After all, wasn't that why she broke up with me in the first place? Because I had been a pig?

"How's the Anderson Cottage?" she had asked.

"Great," I had answered, keeping my eyes on the water. "Would be better if you were there."

"Oh, Art," she sighed. "You have to stop trying so hard."

With that, she strutted right on by, flashing her bikini body at me like bait on a fishhook. I shook my head in frustration. What exactly did Gloria want from me? She didn't want to be with me, but she needed my attention. I sighed and wondered if I would ever understand women.

An ear-piercing whistle blasted through my thoughts, and I began scanning the open water immediately.

"Help!" a woman shrieked from shore. "That girl is drowning!"

I skyrocketed down from the lifeguard chair, grabbed the emergency board, and sprinted in the direction of the cry for help.

"Help!" I heard again. Elizabeth Chase, the girl from the second floor, jumped up and down, waving frantically at me. "It's Katie!" she wailed. "Katie is out there… She was here one minute and pulled out the next. You need to help her, please!"

I felt my heart beating from inside my chest, because the truth was, in the years I had been a lifeguard, never had I actually had to save anybody's life. I looked over my shoulder at the other lifeguards, who were busy retrieving children and swimmers taken captive by the enormous swells and fierce riptide, none of them able to help Katie Roy.

I could see the outline of Katie's bobbing head and prayed to God that she was a strong swimmer, because she was at least one hundred yards from shore. I dropped down on the board and paddled as fast and hard as I could, working with all my might, watching Katie bob up and down in the deep ocean water and relieved every time she jumped up and was able to take another breath.

"Swim to the side!" I called out. "You can get out of the riptide if you swim horizontally."

If Katie heard me, she didn't understand. Her wet hair covered her eyes, and her expression was that of sheer panic.

"Help!" she called out as I finally approached her. "Please!"

"It's okay. Everything is going to be okay." I rolled off the board and grabbed her trembling body with one arm. Her face was blue, like she had been struggling for air for a bit.

"Grab on," I instructed. She placed her hands on either side of the board, and I scooted her on top, shimmying close behind.

"Art," she gasped between breaths.

"Just hold on," I instructed. "You're going to be okay."

Her breathing was heavy, like she still couldn't inhale fully. I kicked through the riptide, allowing an incoming wave to crash over us. "Are you okay?" I asked, placing my hand on her cold, trembling shoulder. She stuck her face to the board, closed her eyes, and cried. "My father is going to kill me," she wailed, grabbing onto my hand with hers.

The hand-holding caught me off guard, and between the adrenaline pumping through my veins and the fact that being this close to Katie made me feel something I had never felt before, I decided it would be best to let go of her hand and utilize my body to get us safely to shore.

"Thank you, Art," she whispered from beneath me. "You're my hero."

CHAPTER SIXTEEN- 1959

KATIE

*M*y hand trembled nervously as I knocked on the door of the Anderson Cottage, first floor. It had been two days since Art had saved me. What had started as the most embarrassing moment in my life had turned into the most romantic. As long as I lived, I didn't think I would ever forget the feeling that washed over me as Art lifted me effortlessly onto his surfboard and paddled us to safety.

I thought for sure that my father was going to snatch me up and take me home when he found out about the near-drowning incident. Imagine my surprise when instead, he asked for the name of the lifeguard who rescued me. I explained that it was Arthur Young, the boy from the first floor. "Well then, we need to have him over for dinner to thank him. And in the future, Katie, only go up to here," he said sternly, gesturing toward his waist.

I was just about to walk away from Art's door when he answered, obviously just getting out of the shower, wearing nothing but a towel. I tried to keep my eyes focused on his eyes, but those stubborn things kept wandering to his chest, his waist, his towel, and back up again. I felt the blood rush to my cheeks and did my best to act cool. "Art," I declared, like I was announcing the royal family.

"Katie," he responded, slight amusement in his tone.

"I... we... wanted to thank you, for what you did."

"Just doing my job, Katie Roy."

My heart fluttered, and my knees grew weak. I had never been so close to a man wearing only a towel. Especially a man as handsome as Art.

"Yes," I began. "I understand that. My father would like to have you over for dinner... to thank you... tonight."

His eyes landed on mine, and I rubbed my arms nervously. "My father... he's really strict. You see, my sister... she drowned in a pool when I was a baby..." I knew I was rambling, and I noticed he'd started to take pity on me, on my story.

"What time is dinner?" Art asked. "I'm actually really hungry."

"We will be on the second floor, with Elizabeth and the Chase family," I explained.

"What time?"

"Six thirty? We are having pot roast."

"See you then, Katie Roy."

* * *

AT SIX THIRTY SHARP, Art Young knocked on the door. I heard my mother welcome him inside as I double-checked my outfit in the mirror of Elizabeth's bedroom. I had considered wearing my favorite blue-and-white-pinstriped dress but had settled on my pink one-piece shirtwaist-style playsuit, one of my favorite outfits. I pulled my hair back in a ponytail and ran my fingers through my bangs.

"He's here!" Elizabeth squealed from the doorway.

"Is my lipstick okay?" I asked.

"Your lipstick is perfect. He looks *so* handsome, Katie."

I smiled and nodded, leaving her bedroom, convinced that Art could show up to dinner in a towel and he would look magnificent.

"Hi, everyone," I called out as I made my way into the living room. Mr. Chase sat in a brown-and-tan plaid armchair, and my father and Art were already seated on the adjacent couch. Mrs. Chase and my mother were busy in the kitchen as Elizabeth eagerly set the table.

"Katie," my father called out. "We were just talking about you. Come greet the boy—the man who saved your life. We are forever grateful."

I nodded and approached Art, who rose to his feet from the plaid sofa. Elizabeth wasn't wrong. He looked snazzy in his red shorts and his blue-and-white-striped colored shirt. His usual mess of blond hair was slicked back neatly, causing him to look even older than he already did.

"Thank you," I said, taking his hand in mine. "Thank you for what you did."

"Cigars, gentlemen?" my father invited.

"Oh, Norman," my mom pleaded. "Wait until after dinner. The roast is ready."

I caught Art's eye and smiled, as he hadn't yet let go of my hand. I looked from his eyes to my hand and back up again. Finally, after what felt like ten years, he removed his hand from mine, and I wished more than anything he would hold it again.

* * *

"THAT WAS SOME DINNER," Art declared, rubbing his belly, as we crossed the street onto Long Sands Beach. I was shocked when my parents agreed to let me take a walk after dinner with Art. After all, the sun was setting, and it would be dark out in no time. But I wasn't going to question it.

"Mrs. Chase is an excellent cook," I agreed.

It was low tide, and the water seemed to extend out toward the horizon for what seemed like miles. "The sky is so beautiful," I said, kicking through the sand and making my way toward the edge of the shallow water. The sky looked like a watercolor painting in shades of pink, orange, and purple, and the setting sun reflected off the water in ways I had only seen in the movies. "It's breathtaking," I added, staring out at the scene.

"It sure is," Art agreed.

His hands were in the pockets of his stylish red shorts, and he shook his head in admiration... of... me?

"What is it?" I asked, suddenly confused.

He took a couple of steps toward me and took my hands in his. "You," he whispered. "You are beautiful, Katie. Simply... I don't know... breathtaking."

I laughed out loud, and I could tell this caught him off guard. "Me? Breathtaking? I'm a lot of things, Arthur Young, but breathtaking is not one of them."

"Well... I beg to differ," he said confidently.

"Oh yeah?"

"Yeah."

"I haven't been getting that impression," I stated, more boldly than I meant to.

"What do you mean?"

"You've avoided me like the plague. You won't take me surfing. You referred to me as an 'ankle biter.'"

He let go of my hands and placed them on my shoulders. "I'm sorry about that. I-I'm just trying to do the right thing."

"The right thing?"

"Yes, the right thing. How old are you? Fifteen?"

"I'll be sixteen next week," I announced proudly, stepping

closer to him. I could feel his breath against my cheek, and I wanted to be closer.

"I'm seventeen, turning eighteen in August. It's just... fifteen is *young*, Katie."

"Fifteen is young," I affirmed, placing my arms around his lower back, surprising myself with my sauciness. "But I'm turning sixteen next week. So for one month, I will be sixteen and you will be seventeen. I, for one, don't see anything wrong with that." I leaned in and kissed his cheek, pausing to leave my mouth against his skin for an extra second.

"It's not *you* I'm worried about," he whispered, a tiny bit breathless.

"My father?"

"Yes, your father."

"He's harmless," I reassured, leaning forward and kissing his other cheek.

We stood there, inches apart in the setting sun, eyes locked, until there was only us and the moonlight. And it was then that Art Young took my face in his strong hands and kissed my lips, in the deepest, most passionate kiss of my entire life.

CHAPTER SEVENTEEN- NOW

MAGGIE

ONE WEEK BEFORE THE BIG DAY

I have been dreading this moment since last night. The front door is the only way to access my office from the parking lot, and that means being face-to-face with Seth, the man I humiliated and who in turn humiliated me. I take a deep breath and reach for the door handle, and sure enough, it flies open before I can make contact.

"Good morning, Miss Thatcher." Seth smiles.

My heart sinks, and I'm not sure why. "Good morning, Seth," I say as I brush past him like I do each morning; only this time, I don't make eye contact. I just can't.

"Have a great day, Miss Thatcher," he calls to me, but I am already heading down the hallway toward my office, and I just don't have the heart to look back.

I'm not a terrible person... right? Clearly, Seth had to know that last night's arrangement would have been nothing more than physical. He had to know by now that I was too emotionally screwed up to have any sort of relationship. But in some ways, he isn't wrong. I need to sort through my feelings about West Young, because he is getting *married*. And there is a piece of me that does want to be with Seth. We had a great couple of years together, Seth and I. He seemed to understand me in a way that other men didn't, which was both a blessing and a curse.

I bypass my office this morning and march right down the hall toward the elevators to assisted living. I lost a lot of sleep last night, some of that due to the embarrassment of calling out West's name instead of Seth's but also because I was worried about Art. I take the elevator to the third floor and continue down the corridor until I approach his apartment.

"Art." I knock. "Art, it's me, Maggie."

"I'm not coming out," Art calls from inside.

"That's fine. But could you let me in?"

"Okay, Maggie," he says from inside. He opens the door and allows me into his small home. Empty food containers line his counter, along with wine bottles and dirty wine glasses.

"Looks like you had a party," I joke.

Art stands there, in his living room, wearing only a T-shirt and his boxer shorts. He clearly hasn't showered or shaved. "Funny, Maggie. You should be a comedian."

* * *

IT TAKES about an hour and two cups of coffee before Art begins to open up. We talk about his friend Kathryn—Katie for short. He explains that although he married his wife Gloria and had a wonderful life with her, it was Katie Roy that was the love of his life. His soulmate.

"Did she ever marry?" I ask, confused. If she was the love of his life, why wouldn't he have married her?

Art stared at me for a beat, his eyes lost in a world of sadness. "Speaking of love lost, have you talked to Westly about the wedding?"

"Ugh," I moaned. "That's totally out of my control, and you know it." I grab my berry lipstick out of my purse and apply it to my pouting lips.

"You need to tell him how you feel, Maggie."

"I did."

"When?"

"I don't know... back in 2010? When I ruined his life?"

"Take it from me," he says with a sigh. "If Westly is your soulmate, you can't let him go."

I LEAVE Art in his room with the donut I purchased for him on the way to work. I intend on pressing the elevator button for the lobby, but something stops me. Instead, I press the button for the fifth floor. I don't go to the fifth floor often, but something inside me is tugging me to visit my nursing home friends.

I exit the elevator on floor five and make my way toward room 506 to visit one of my favorite patients, Gwendoline Ellis, but I am stopped at her door by her husband, Joey Chase.

"Maggie Thatcher," Joey exclaims, stopping to kiss me on the forehead. "How are you, dear?"

"I'm good," I lie.

He studies me and reads me like a book. "How are you, really?"

"Let's just say I was looking to see my old friend Gwendoline. I was looking for some advice."

"She's getting washed up now," he explains. "She should be done in a few."

"Would you mind doing me a favor?" I ask, realizing that this is something I usually don't ask anyone. "Would you mind checking in on Art? He's really shaken up. We had a visitor yesterday—Kathryn Roy—and Art has been beside himself since."

"Katie Roy came here?" Joey asks, wide-eyed.

"Yes, she said her name was Kathryn—"

"What room is he in? I will go see him now."

"Room 206."

"Thank you. Could you tell Gwendoline that I will be right back?"

"Of course," I answer, taking a seat outside of Gwendoline's room, wondering what on Earth could possibly have gone down between Art Young and Kathryn Roy.

* * *

"Come in," Gwendoline calls from her bed.

"Hi, it's me, Maggie Thatcher," I sing.

"Oh, Maggie, hello, dear."

"I… I miss our talks, Gwendoline, and I could really use some advice."

She is sitting up in her bed, a fresh steamy cup of tea in her hand. "I would love some company," she admits.

"Oh, good," I say, pulling up a chair next to her. Her silver hair is pulled up in a twist on the top of her head. I wonder to myself just how old she is now—she must be approaching one hundred and two.

"It's about Westly," I explain.

"Art's grandson?"

"Yes."

"You are friends with him still?"

"Yes, but that's the problem, Gwendoline. I want—I need it to be *more* than that. We are more than friends, and I've been lying to myself all these years. I've been pretending that I can stay friends with him, but I love him… so much." I don't expect the tears that begin streaming down my cheeks, and

Gwendoline hands me a tissue. "I just thought... maybe you have some advice?"

She thinks for a minute. "Why aren't you together?"

"Because," I start. "Because of a stupid promise we made to each other when we were teenagers. I did something, bad, and he was so mad at me. He wanted me out of his life, but he told me if I promised to only be his friend that I could be in his life. But now he's getting married, and I can't keep a relationship to save my life—"

"Married?"

"Yes," I wail. "He's getting married in a week."

"And you want to be with him?" she asks, her voice slow and steady.

"Yes."

"You need to tell him that, dear."

"But I made a promise," I whine.

"Let me ask you something, Maggie. Is this really about a promise you made to Westly? Or a promise you made to yourself? Sometimes, we need to do some soul-searching to understand what is really happening."

"What do you mean?"

"You will understand in time, dear. I made a lot of mistakes when I was a teenager," she says. "But I grew from those mistakes. Nobody deserves to be punished for them in this way. You deserve an opportunity to be with him, Maggie. You deserve a chance to fight."

CHAPTER EIGHTEEN-1959

ART

Katie Roy. Her name rolled off the tip of my tongue with ease. If I was having a bad day, I simply whispered her name, and the tension in my body seemed to simply fade away. It had been weeks since Katie's sixteenth birthday, and I couldn't get enough of her.

What had started as walks on the beach here and there had quickly turned into more. Although I was still overly intimated by her father, I didn't see any harm in taking oceanside strolls. We grew accustomed to walking, hand in hand, down the long stretch of sand while the day turned into night. And it was then, in the glow of the moonlight under the starry sky, that we would kiss.

I had even caved and taken her surfing. She picked it up faster than I thought she would. She had lain down on my yellow surfboard, looking tiny in comparison to its length, and I had pushed the board forward and hollered, "Paddle! Paddle, Katie!" It had taken her two or three tries, but after a couple of wipeouts, she was surfing. Happiness beamed off her in ways I couldn't explain. I wasn't used to being able to make a person so happy, but with Katie, it came easily.

There I stood, at the storm door of the Anderson Cottage, third floor. Dressed in my best shirt and trousers, waiting to pick Katie up for our first official date. I chewed on my bottom lip and breathed in nervously. A bouquet of flowers was hidden behind my back.

"Art!" she squealed as she answered the door. "Art, come in."

"I got these for you," I told her as I handed her the flowers.

She had curled her hair and applied more makeup than I was used to seeing her wear, but she looked stunning. "I love them, thank you," she said. I followed her inside, her blue-and-white-pinstriped dress puffing up around her as she spun around. "I'm just going to put them in some water."

I nodded and stuck my hands in my pockets, waiting for her return.

"Art!" a voice called from the sitting room. It was Norman Roy, and my heart began to race. Of course he was not going to make this easy on me.

"Big date tonight, eh?" he asked, cigar hanging out of the side of his mouth. He was holding a newspaper in front of him, but his gaze was steady on me.

"Yes, sir. I'm taking Katie roller skating."

"Sounds lovely."

"It will be, sir."

Mr. Roy folded the newspaper up and placed it on the table next to him. He puffed on his cigar and exhaled for a beat. "Katie," he started. "She's the most important thing in the world."

"Of course," I agreed. "I'll take good care of her, sir."

"I'm ready!" Katie announced as she skipped into the sitting room, her mother following closely behind.

"Norman," Mrs. Roy said, "are you giving this handsome young man a hard time?"

"Never." He chuckled. "I was just telling him how important Katie is to me."

"Oh, Daddy," Katie cried. "So embarrassing. We will be fine."

Katie kissed her parents and headed for the door. "Let's go, Art. Roller skating awaits."

* * *

IT HAD BEEN the perfect evening. It turned out that Katie Roy loved to roller skate. She even knew how to skate backward, which was impressive because I, for one, could barely stay upright on my skates.

When the last song played, we held hands and skated around the rink. Her smile was as bright as the sun. "I don't want this night to end," she had cried out.

"Me neither," I replied. "Don't I need to get you home?"

She had shaken her head. "It's fine. We can drive up to the Nubble... I've always wanted to do that. And then we can head home."

In hindsight, I wished that I had trusted my instinct and taken her home. Instead, we drove over to the Nubble Lighthouse. I had never seen it lit up at night and found myself captivated by the way it seemed to tower over us, high up on a hill, under the twinkling stars. We parked, staring down through the windshield at what felt like a mountain of rocks, and I gazed in awe as the waves crashed over the rocky shore. Katie snuggled against me, and for that moment, we felt like the only two people on the planet.

"I had so much fun tonight, Art. Thank you."

"I had fun with you, too."

I used my fingers to find her chin in the darkness, then her cheeks, and her mouth, as her face was only a shadow in the night. I pulled her close to me until our lips met—a kiss that we had shared in the past but this time felt like more.

"Art," she whispered, pulling me closer. Her hands grabbed my shoulders, and she nodded to the back seat of my car.

"Come here," I said, climbing into the back, and she followed. I lay back and pulled her over me, grabbing her lower back and kissing her lips like it was our last night on Earth. "We should probably get back soon," I suggested between breaths, only stopping now was not my preference. I could have kissed Katie all night if it were up to me.

She climbed on top of me and began unbuttoning my shirt. I knew better—really, I did. But I had also never been so captivated by anyone. And Katie was removing my shirt and kissing me in all the right places. It was only when she started unbuttoning her own dress that I held my hand up for her to stop.

"Why?" she asked, obviously hurt.

"It's too fast," I explained. *And I'm scared to death of your father,* I wanted to add.

As if on cue, Katie and I became blinded by a bright-yellow light accompanied by banging on the back window of my car.

"Kathryn Roy!" her father called from outside the car, shining his flashlight through the window, revealing Katie straddling me in the back seat of my car, me shirtless and her with her dress unbuttoned from the waist up. I threw my head back against the seat and covered my eyes with my hands. "Kathryn Roy!" he called again. "You come out here this instant."

CHAPTER NINETEEN-1959

KATIE

I had often wondered what it would feel like to have a broken heart. There was a part of me that was relieved; now that I knew what it felt like, could I get on with my life and stop anticipating? Although I wanted the answer to be yes, I knew that wasn't the truth, because the hole I had in my heart for Arthur Young was bigger than the span of the Atlantic Ocean. I wanted to be with him more than anything, but my father was *not* having it.

I tried to explain to him that breaking curfew was my fault, not Art's. When he asked about the kissing in the car, I also tried to take responsibility for how fast we had moved, but that just made my father angrier. Weeks had gone by since our date, and I was only allowed out of the cottage with Elizabeth, during the day. I tried to enjoy my time with her, really, I did. But it didn't matter whether we were lying on our beach towels or splashing in the waves; I was fixated on Art. Was he lifeguarding? Was he watching me? Did he miss me?

It was difficult enough knowing that he was living on the first floor and I the third. If we bumped into each other outside of the Anderson Cottage, he simply smiled and waved. I didn't blame him for this; my father could be frightening. I had begged and pleaded with him to *please*, just give me one more chance, but he wouldn't budge.

That is why I had to take matters into my own hands. It was my idea to send Elizabeth down to the first floor that Friday evening with a note for Art. *7:00 p.m., first floor,* I had scribbled on the tiny piece of paper. I knew it was risky, but my parents had plans with the Chase family on the second floor that night. I also had an inkling that they would be up late, as my father purchased a new bottle of whisky along with his favorite cigars.

I had waited at Elizabeth's bedroom window for Art. He typically finished his shift at the beach at 5:00 p.m. and, if he didn't surf afterward, would come right home. Sure enough, at 5:15, Art crossed the street from Long Sands Beach and entered the Anderson Cottage on the first floor.

"Go now!" I instructed Elizabeth. She complied, skipping down the back porch steps of the gray cottage at the speed of light. She caught Art as he was leaning his surfboard against the outside of the cottage and tucked the rolled-up piece of paper in his hand before he could even mutter a hello.

Sure enough, my parents had asked if I would be joining them for dinner at 6:30pm with the Chase family on the second floor. "I'm not feeling up for it," I had explained. "I'm going to get to bed early." I had waited for them to head downstairs for dinner before stuffing a bunch of blankets under the brown-and-orange afghan on my bed, hopeful it would look like I was sleeping if someone checked on me. I crept out the storm door on the third floor and checked the clock, which read 6:58 p.m. I crawled down the stairs of the Anderson Cottage, listening carefully for my parents' voices. Elizabeth had planned to join them for dinner, eager to distract them in any way she possibly could. I listened closely to the usual laughter of Gwendoline and my mother, accompanied by the deep voices of Joey Chase and my father, echoing through the still night air alongside the familiar cloud of cigar smoke that wafted from within.

I took a deep breath and scurried by the storm door of the second floor. If I was going to get caught, that would surely be the time. I leaned against the cottage and waited, but the typical banter of my parents with their friends carried on. "Okay," I whispered to myself. "Here goes nothing."

I dashed down the remaining stairs of the Anderson Cottage and quietly tiptoed over to the door of the first floor. "Art," I whispered. "Art, it's me. Let me in." I tried to hide the desperation in my voice, but it was nearly impossible.

The storm door flew open, and Art gathered me in his arms, relief flooding over me like the ocean water on a hot and muggy day. "Katie," he whispered, pulling me close. "Are you all right?"

"I'm all right now."

"Are you wearing a nightgown?" He chuckled.

I nodded in embarrassment. "I told my parents I was going to sleep."

"You're crazy, you know that?"

We scampered down the hallway to his bedroom, closing the door behind us and pulling the window shade down. Art sat down on his bed, and I followed, kissing him before he was able to get a word in.

"I've missed you," he confessed between breaths.

"I've missed you so much."

He lay down on his bed, and I curled up next to him, resting my head in the crook of his neck. "I hate that we can't be together," he said in the darkness. The anguish in his voice broke my heart.

"We can make it work," I insisted. "My father—he will come around."

"I hope you're right, Katie." Art was quiet for a moment before kissing my forehead, my nose, my cheek, and then my lips. I hadn't intended to come downstairs for this purpose. I had only wanted to talk. But there, in the darkness, alone with Art Young in the privacy of his bedroom, all bets were off. I pulled him on top of me, allowing him to flood my face and neck with kisses.

"Art," I gasped in the darkness of his bedroom. "Art... I think I love you."

"I love you, too, Katie Roy."

He rolled over, and I climbed on top of him as our lips danced together in the moonlight. He pulled my nightgown over my head, and I removed his shirt. The feeling of his skin against mine was invigorating. I was engrossed with Arthur Young... all of him. Every touch and every movement were invigorating. Nothing else mattered in the world as long as we could be together.

"Did you hear something?" Art asked, his eyes jolting open.

"No," I moaned, bringing his face close to mine once more.

"No, Katie—I heard something."

I pulled myself off him and listened carefully, determined to believe that Art was being paranoid. But I knew in my gut he was right.

"Katie!" a voice called from Art's window.

"Elizabeth!" I cried, reaching for my nightgown and scurrying over to the window.

"Katie. They know you're gone. And your dad. He's had a lot to drink. He's on his way downstairs."

"Oh no," I shrieked, tossing my nightgown over my head.

"You can go out the window, Katie. Go... now," Art

instructed as he buttoned his shirt back up. Our conversation was interrupted by the pounding on Art's front door. Art pulled me over to the window and began removing the screen. "Go out this way. He won't know you're here."

"Kathryn!" my father called. "Kathryn Roy, I know you're in there!"

"Come out this way," Elizabeth called. "Quick!"

My knees trembled, and my body froze. "I-I can't. He already knows. I-I'm so sorry, Art. I shouldn't have come here."

A loud crash, and I realized my father was inside the cottage, making his way to Art's bedroom. I did the only thing I could do in the moment: crumble into a ball on the bedroom floor and cover my eyes, because my father was a complete monster when he drank too much.

"Betty!" my father called, thrusting open the door harder than necessary. Art hopped up from his bed and raised his hands in surrender. "I told you to *stay away from her!*" he roared.

"Daddy!" I cried out. "Daddy, I'm not Betty—I'm *Katie*. Betty is... she's dead! We were just talking! Leave him alone."

Joey Chase appeared in the doorway, my mother following closely behind. "Norman," Joey called. "Norman, let's go back inside and figure this out tomorrow."

My father's face turned crimson as he charged toward Art. My father grabbed him by the throat and pinned him against the wall. It all happened rather fast, and I knew in the back of my mind that if Arthur wanted to defend himself, surely, he could have; he simply didn't have it in his heart to hurt my father.

"I told you to stay away from her," he shrilled.

"Let him go!" I cried, rushing toward the bedroom door, where my mother stood, mouth gaping. "Mommy, make him stop!"

STACY LEE

"Norman Roy, you stop that this instant," she said sternly.

But my father didn't stop. He pulled his fist back and pounded on Art's face, one after another after another, until Joey Chase came to his rescue. Art fell to the floor, blood gushing from his nose and mouth, the pain in his eyes too much to bear.

"You go on upstairs," Joey said to me. "Go on home, and I will take care of Arthur."

I complied, tears gushing down the sides of my face, my heart breaking into a billion pieces.

* * *

I PACKED the last item in my suitcase and zipped it closed. It was only the second week in August, and we were supposed to have two more weeks at the Anderson Cottage. But because my father couldn't trust me around Art, and most likely because he was feeling shame for his behavior (rightfully so), my parents and I were packing up and heading back to Boston early. I only had one more night at the Anderson Cottage before heading back home.

I hadn't seen Art since the night of the incident. Any piece of me that was determined to sneak downstairs to be with him had diminished. Mostly because I was afraid for him—watching my father punch him repeatedly was something I would never be able to erase from my mind. And then there was my father's remorse. He had come to me the next morning, wanting to have a heart-to-heart. He had explained how hard it had been for my mother and him to lose my sister. He needed me to understand that I was all they had left.

"Promise me, Katie," he had pleaded. "Promise me that you will trust me. I know what's best for you... never in a billion years will you *ever* be with that boy again."

I had nodded in agreement, mostly because I loved my

parents more than anything in the world but also because I wanted to keep him away from Art. "I promise," I had declared between tears. "I trust you, and you know what's best. But if it's okay with you, can I just say goodbye?"

It had been a long shot for sure, but my mother convinced him to let me say farewell to Art Young. I had found him that morning, wading waist-deep in the ocean on Long Sands, allowing the waves to collapse over him, one after another.

"Nice day for a swim?" I had asked.

He shot up from the water like a bullet being released from a gun. "Katie," he cried. "Joey told me you left."

I kicked through the water, holding my dress up, trying to avoid being splashed by the incoming waves. "We are leaving today."

Our eyes locked, and for the first time, I noticed his black eyes and swollen nose. "Your nose…"

Art smiled and laid back in the water, floating effortlessly over each wave. "My face will survive," he admitted. "But my heart, Katie… my broken heart, that's another story."

I watched him float over the waves like a buoy, and I realized at that moment that Art Young was going to be all right. Art had the sea, and even though his heart was breaking, as was mine, he would be okay if he had the ocean—and nobody, not even my father, could take that from him.

"I'm leaving now," I declared more firmly than necessary. "I'm not allowed to phone you or write to you. My father, he said… that never in a billion years can we be together. But I want you to know, I *do* love you… and I probably always will."

If Art heard me, he chose to ignore me. His sun-kissed hair floated around him, his eyes closed and his smile the same smile from the day we first met. "Swim with me, Katie," he pleaded. "Swim with your old pal Art."

"I'm not wearing a bathing suit." I chuckled. "You want me to swim in my clothes?"

"It's not a crime to swim in your clothes, is it?"

"I suppose not, but my father might not like it."

"We've been through enough together, Katie Roy. I think we will be okay."

With that, I sank into the oncoming tide, my favorite skirt surrounding me like a parachute as I reached for Art's hand.

"Do you believe in soulmates?" Art asked, his voice both calm and smooth.

"I didn't before," I admitted. "But I think I do now."

We floated there together, Art and I, soaking in the serenity of the sea and each other, until the last possible second, like they were our last moments on Earth.

PART THREE

CHAPTER TWENTY- NOW

MAGGIE

THREE DAYS BEFORE THE BIG DAY

I shut my laptop and unplug it from the charger, relieved that I am caught up on my work. I fly out to Arizona in less than twenty-four hours, and if nothing else, I can rest assured that the residents at WVC will have enough activities to keep them occupied—or at least out of trouble until I return next week.

Although I am ready to leave for the evening, I find it critical to check on Art prior to my departure. I asked him if he wanted to fly out to Arizona with me for West's wedding. "Why would I fly across the country to watch my grandson make the biggest mistake of his life?" he barked. "*You* are the one he should be marrying."

I hated when Art spoke this way, but I knew he was right. I march down the hallway toward the elevators and press the button for the second floor. When I exit the elevator, I am overly surprised to see Joey Chase standing outside Art's door.

"Hi, Joey," I say, hugging him around the shoulders. "You here to see Art?"

"More like trying to talk some sense into him," he huffs.

"Did you know that Katie Roy is moving into assisted living and Art is doing nothing about it?"

"I can hear you!" Art shouts from inside. "That ship sailed many moons ago. If you were going to do something about it then you should have helped me knock that father of hers out cold the night he attacked me."

"What is he talking about?" I ask in confusion.

"Art, open the door. Maggie is here, and she wants to talk to you."

The door creaks open, and Joey shuffles into Art's apartment with me following closely behind.

"What is this about—Katie?" I ask Art, who is once again surrounded by empty takeout containers, open bags of chips, and dirty wine glasses—all clear indicators of a broken heart.

"Are you having a nice pity party?" Joey asks.

"Now, why would I be having a pity party?"

"Because you lost the love of your life back in 1959. I was there. I witnessed it."

"The love of my life was Gloria Young, thank you very much. My wife of thirty-five years."

I nod in agreement. "Art lost Gloria in the late nineties."

"I know that," Joey states calmly. "But I'm not talking about Gloria."

I study Art in confusion. "Art, what happened with this Katie back in 1959?"

"Oh, the two of you are going to be the death of me," Art moans. "I fell in love with Katie Roy back in the late fifties, early sixties, yes. Her father hated my guts and beat the crap out of me—end of story."

"No!" Joey shouts, surprising us both. "Not end of story! She just moved *in*! She lives down the hall from you! All you have to do is go talk to her."

"Why do you suppose Art should talk with her?" I ask, suddenly very curious about Kathryn Roy.

"Because she was his *soulmate.* He told me himself."

"Come on, now, Joey. Just because you helped me ice my nose and find my teeth after Katie's dad almost murdered me doesn't mean you get to hold what I said about her against me over sixty years later, does it?"

I sit down on the couch next to Art and wrap my arm around his shoulder. "If she was your soulmate, then why didn't you end up together?" I wondered if it was obvious that I was asking for my own personal reasons.

"She made a promise to her father," he explained. "Never in a billion years would she get back together with me."

I jump to my feet. "What did you just say?" My question sounds more urgent than I meant it to. "Never in a what?"

Art rolls his eyes. "Never in a *billion* years," he repeats.

"Has… did you ever…" My voice trails off. Was this expression something West had heard his grandfather say? After all these years, I thought I was holding onto a promise that was near and dear to West's heart, when it was really Art's baggage? "Did you ever tell that story to West?" I shout, the volume of my voice no longer under my control.

He thinks for a moment. "Probably," he confesses. "But it was a long time ago, Maggie."

I shove my face in my hands and take slow breaths. "That is what West asked me to promise him. Never in a billion years could we be together."

Joey and Grandpa stare at me in silence. "And now I get to go watch him marry Natalia the supermodel," I finish. "Some happily ever after I get."

"Did you read Gwendoline's blog this week?" Joey asks.

I shake my head in confusion. "What do you mean, Gwendoline's blog?"

"Sorry," he chuckles. "I forget sometimes that she is anonymous. She writes the blogs for the WVC website under the name Miss Taken. Get it—she's taken, and she's misunderstood. Kind of a funny play on words..." His voice trails off.

I grab my cell phone and pull up the WVC website, my mind blown that I never realized Gwendoline Chase was Miss Taken. I pull up her blog and read it slowly, realizing with every word that Gwendoline was speaking directly to me, in response to the conversation I had with her in her room last week.

DEFINITION OF NEVER/NOT *in a thousand/million/billion years—*
*used as a strong way of saying that something is **extremely unlikely or impossible**. —Merriam Webster*

IMPOSSIBLE. *Such a crummy word. The mere principle of identifying something as extremely unlikely, or not going to happen, disturbs me in ways that are unexplainable. I often come across as overly optimistic, naïve, or even childish at times, simply because I truly believe that nothing is unattainable or unsolvable; there is simply always a way.*

Consider the New England Patriots in Superbowl XLIX. My party guests vanished back to the comfort of their own sofas long before the end of the game. Although I insisted that two minutes was plenty of time to pull around, they disagreed, leaving me to witness the greatest comeback of all time unfold before my very eyes—victory.

A simple Google search will reveal concepts throughout history that were once considered impossible. Automobiles, lightbulbs, air travel, television, and computers for starters. I sometimes chuckle to myself when I think of the satisfaction that must have amounted when award-winning inventors or well-educated scientists stared down their critics in the eyes with glee and gloated, "Told you so." And what about those that allowed their dreams and greatest desires to be oppressed by others? Imagine the billions of ideas, successes, and relationships that could have been.

So, if that's the case and impossible things can be possible, then why is it that we get so irrationally stuck and paralyzed with fear when we consider what we desire to be unlikely, impossible, or in simpler terms... not going to happen? I, for one, will jiggle that Magic 8-Ball until as I see it, YES, appears in the blue triangle, securing my destiny in my own hands.

What I hope you can take from today's article, dear reader, is never give up hope. Just because the thing (or person, for that matter) you desire seems remarkably out of reach doesn't mean it can't happen. The only thing worse than giving up hope on something you want more than anything... is regret.

"Never in a million years will that happen," you say... never in a billion? Well, my friends, you just might be that one in a billion. Never give up hope.

Until Next Time,
   Miss Taken
   Xoxoxoxoxo

Art stares up at me in awe, and I can't remove my gaze from the page.

"She's not wrong," I admit under my breath. For all this time, have I been using the silly promise I made to West back in 2010 as a shield for my true feelings? So what if I practically ruined his life for a few years? And even though I screwed up big-time, didn't I help him find his mother? I know that West was hurt that night, but if I really, truly wanted our friendship to be more than that, couldn't I do something about it? How have I been settling for anything less all these years? The mere fact that I haven't been able to hold a relationship with anyone else speaks volumes, doesn't it? This is what Gwendoline was referring to. If I were to honor the preposterous promise I made to West, would I have even had the guts to pursue him? Up until now, the answer has been *no*. My problem hasn't been with West Young and a silly little contract we made over ten years ago; my problem has always been with *myself.*

"I have to go."

"Where are you going?" Art asks, taking my hand in his.

"I'm going to tell West that I love him—I'm going to tell him he's my soulmate," I say boldly. *"Don't* tell him I'm coming." I point my finger at Art like he is a child in time out. "And, Art?"

"Yes?"

"I think you should do the same with Katie Roy."

CHAPTER TWENTY-ONE-NOW

MAGGIE

48 HOURS BEFORE THE BIG DAY

*M*y plane touches down in Phoenix earlier than expected. I chug the last sip of my third Tito's and soda and peek out my window. It has been a six-hour flight, but it felt like six years. I binge-watched old episodes of *Carolina Sands* on Netflix, something I hadn't done in a while, the whole time searching Silva Flores's features and mannerisms for signs of West's signature traits.

I gather my luggage from the overhead compartment and bolt down the boarding bridge, into the airport, and into my Uber. I give the driver West's home address, the only address I have for him. He isn't expecting me until tomorrow, when I am due to arrive for the wedding, and I silently hope he will be home, preferably *not* with Natalia.

I study the desert scenery as we zoom by, and I instantly understand what West has been raving about all these years, as it is truly breathtaking. As we arrive at a red light, my mouth gapes in awe at a six-foot cactus perched on the median. "Is that real?" I ask the Uber driver in disbelief.

"Is what real?"

"That cactus."

"Yes, ma'am. It is very real."

"That's freaking amazing," I say, snapping a photo with my cell phone. "And that? Is that Camelback Mountain?"

"Yes, ma'am," he says again.

I gaze at the large stretch of earth and giggle. "He's right," I say. "It does look like giant anthills." At this point, the Uber driver is absently nodding his head at my ridiculous commentary, but I could care less. The adrenaline pumping through my veins at full speed is not only taking over my jet lag but also helping me survive this moment, because what I am about to do is probably the wildest thing I will have ever done. I swipe open my texts, realizing that I have forgotten to notify Jordan of my arrival.

Maggie: *Landed. In the Uber now.*

Jordan: *OMG Maggie. You've got this. You are so brave.*

Jordan is right; to pull off what I am about to do, I need to be brave. At this point, crossing a rocky ocean chasm seems easier than confronting West. I lean my head back and think about him—that first summer we met on the private beach at WVC, all the deep conversations we had with each other, how he is still, to this day, the only one I can completely open up to. And even though things went south and he hated me for a few years, I am pretty sure he still loves me. I'm not sure what is going on with this Natalia business, but I am going to get to the bottom of it. And even if I don't and West turns me away, just like Gwendoline said in her blog, the only thing worse than that would be regret.

The truth is that I have held on to the shame of what I did to West for too long. I need to confront him, and I need to tell him how I truly feel. If I don't, then I will never be able to move on with my life. I think about Seth and the look of defeat in his eyes when I called him another man's name. Is this how I am going to spend the rest of my life? The irony of the situation is almost comical; my best friend is a man I have never been romantically involved with, but I consider him to be the love of my life, while the man I *am* romantically involved with feels more like a friend. I make a mental note to track down a good therapist when I get home; I have a feeling I am going to need one.

"Just about five minutes," the driver says.

I stare out my window at the homes that surround me, and I can't believe how different they are in comparison to those in New England. Everything is completely flat and out in the open, and suddenly, I feel an overwhelming pang of guilt for never coming to visit him prior to this. I glance at my cell phone—7:00 a.m.—and say another silent prayer that not only is West home but that he isn't curled up in bed with his fiancée at the time of my arrival.

MY FINGER TREMBLES as I ring the doorbell to West's house. The nervous feeling in the pit of my stomach has started to encompass my entire being. It's *hot* in Arizona—like, one-hundred- five-degrees hot. I suddenly regret my choice of black leggings and an off-the-shoulder T-shirt. I remove the hair tie from my wrist and scoop my hair off my neck, ringing the bell again.

"Coming!" I hear West call.

I consider running and hiding in the bushes, but that would be ridiculous and highly counterproductive. Instead, I stare straight ahead, take a deep breath, and get ready for the biggest moment of my life.

West flings the door open, an aggravated expression plastered across his tired face, and I realize based on his missing shirt and bedhead that I have, in fact, woken him up. It takes a moment for his eyes to focus, but when he realizes who it is, his demeanor changes.

"What the—"

"Surprise!"

I peer over his shoulder in anticipation of Natalia and her long legs and perfect abs coming up behind him, but if she is home, she is nowhere to be found.

"What the," he says again, reaching down and squeezing me like he's won a prize at the fair. I notice that he hasn't hugged me without a shirt on in years, and temporarily, I have forgotten my name. "I'm sorry—I wasn't expecting you today."

My gaze meets the ground, and I chew my lip. "I know," I say seriously. "I need to talk to you. If you want, we can go somewhere. I don't want to wake up—"

"Oh, Natalia?" he asks as if reading my mind. "She's not here."

"Thank God... I mean, okay..." My voice trails off as he leads me inside, my gaze focused on his shirtless torso and his defined abs, pecs, biceps, and, well... everything I can get a glimpse of, and I am overly thankful that his house has air-conditioning, because I need to cool down, quick.

"Can I get you a coffee or anything?" he asks, tugging me in for another embrace.

I inhale his sweet morning scent, wishing I could bottle it up and take it back home with me. "No, thank you." I plop my backpack on the floor and draw him close to me once more, desperate for this moment to last forever, because in the next couple of seconds, I am either going to make or break our relationship. "I'm actually not staying long," I confess. I stare up at him and wonder what he is thinking. Is he wondering what this means about my involvement in the wedding? Does he know me well enough to already know what I'm going to say?

West crosses his arms over his shirtless chest, and I am completely distracted by his body. I try with all my might to keep eye contact, as I have rehearsed this moment in my mind since I boarded the plane in the middle of the freaking night.

"What's going on, Mags?"

I cross my arms over my own chest, mirroring his body language, and I'm not sure if it's the jet lag or eleven years of being shamed for one stupid mistake, but suddenly, I am *pissed.* "What's going on, *Mags*?" I mimic. "I'll tell you what's going on, West." My voice drips with sass. I step closer to him, so much so that we are inches apart. "You," I say, pointing my finger centimeters from his nose, "are my *soulmate.*"

His mouth curves into a half smile, and his eyebrows rise in that sexy way they always do, and this makes me even angrier. "It's not funny!" I find myself shouting. "You are my soulmate, and I *love* you," I bellow between anxious breaths. I feel my hands begin to tremble, but I clench my fists to my sides, determined to get this out. "I love you. I've always loved you, West. And because of some boneheaded, brainless, stupid, childish thing I did when I was seventeen, I don't get to experience this... this love with you... and not only that, West—I can't experience it with *anybody.* Because at the end of the day, when push comes to shove, I'm not actually capable of being with anyone else... *You're* the only one I want."

West stares down at me, eyes wide, brows furrowed, and I feel bad for a moment because I know this is a lot to take in before coffee. "Maggie..."

I hold up my hand to stop him from continuing. "I'm not done," I state firmly. "I flew across the country today to tell you that *I* think we are supposed to be together. Not just because I think you are freaking hot, because I do... and not because I love you more than life itself, because I do... but because when I can't sleep at night and the whole world is against me, I am able to fall asleep and rest soundly because of you, West. Your voice is the last thing I search for in the back of my mind at night because I know that there is someone in this world who loves me for me, and because of that, I find peace. *You* are the man for me. *You* are the one I want. And I've been hiding behind this stupid promise we made to each other and obsessing over the concept of 'a billion' for over a decade, when the truth is, I was using that promise as an excuse. I needed to find my way, and I finally did. I just wish it wasn't too late."

West opens his mouth to speak, and I don't notice it right away, but he has wrapped his arms around my lower back and is pulling me close to him.

"This whole 'never in a billion' thing, West Young, I'm calling it off. You might say, 'Never in a billion years will we be able to be together'—" I pause, choking back a sob. "But you're *my* one in a billion. I just wish I could be yours."

And just like that, I have said all there is to say. I collapse onto West and his naked chest just as my knees grow weak. The sobs that are now raging from my soul make me want to throw up.

"Maggie," West whispers. "Maggie, it's okay."

"It's not!" I wail. "It's not okay, West." My tears drip down his chest as he holds me tighter.

"Come here," he says. "You need to sit down."

I plop down on his sofa as he disappears into the kitchen and, for the first time, glance around his living room. It's nicer than I expected, and my mind is briefly blown that West keeps his home cleaner than I do, but then the room starts spinning and I begin to panic. *What did I just do?*

He returns with a bottle of water. I receive it eagerly, chugging the whole thing in seconds.

"Thank you," I finally mutter. "I'm sorry for throwing this on you like this, right before the wedding."

West sighs and sits down on the sofa next to me and rubs his face with his hands. "I, uh, I have a confession too," he says slowly.

"A confession?"

"Yeah."

"What are you talking about, West?" I study him, wide-eyed, wondering what on Earth he could possibly be confessing that I haven't already disclosed.

"The wedding, Maggie... there isn't going to be one."

I leap to my feet and begin pacing around the living room. My heart races faster and faster, and my knees grow weak. I slap the palm of my hand against my forehead, a thunderstorm of emotions pumping through my veins. The simple notion of the wedding being called off is too much to process. "I'm sorry...what did you say? What do you mean there isn't going to be a wedding? What happened, West?"

"Well, there was never *actually* a wedding. Like you, I have been torn for the last couple of years about... well, about us."

I stare at him in confusion, unable to process what he is saying. I ease back down onto the sofa and pull my knees to my chest. "I'm not following."

"Maggie, when I fell for you, I fell for you *hard*. And the timing, with Grayson... with my mom... it was all too much to deal with. The promise we made, sure, it meant something back then, but as the years went by and we stayed friends, I always wanted more. I never wanted to just be your friend."

I want to scream at him, but his eyes are those of a sad, lost boy, and I also want to kiss him... I really want to kiss him. "So the wedding...you...you lied to me?" I wait for him to say something more.

"I needed to know how you felt about me. Sure, I could have just asked you, but I *know* you, Maggie, and sometimes, you just say things and you don't even know what you mean."

I shake my head in confusion. "So you lied about the

wedding? Was it, like, a test or something? Or more of a... punishment?"

He sighs, openly frustrated with himself. "I knew you were going to see it that way. It wasn't a test or a punishment but more like an opportunity for you to realize what we have —and what we might lose. Does that make sense?"

I pause for a beat and study my best friend, my *everything*. I want to be mad at him for lying to me, but the truth is he is right. I hid behind a promise we made when we were kids because I didn't want to deal with the feelings we had for each other. I take care of Art like he is my own grandfather partly because it is a piece of West that I can hold onto. Out of context, it was a shitty thing for West to do to me. But based on the circumstances at hand, it was the *only* thing to do. "So you aren't seeing Natalia, then?"

"No." West exhales. "I'm not seeing Natalia."

"And you aren't getting married?"

"No. I'm not getting married."

I rub my hand on his bare knee, suddenly very aware of the powerful emotions I am feeling toward this man, a man I have never even kissed but who knows me better than I know myself. "And you..." My voice trails off again, and I am suddenly overly anxious.

"I love you, Maggie Thatcher. I don't want to be with anyone else. And I think you're freaking hot too."

A piece of me cringes in embarrassment as I reflect on my earlier remark, while the remaining majority of me is ecstatic. I wrap my arms around his neck and squeal. "I love you too."

I haven't realized it until now, but West's hand is on my thigh, a place he has never touched me until now... and I *like* it. Our eyes lock, and I stare into the familiarity of his soul. West traces the bottom of my chin with his finger and guides my mouth towards his in what feels like slow motion. Our lips touch, softly at first and then harder, and I am no longer a prisoner in my own body—I am free. The overwhelming sensation of the love I already have for West in combination with the physical connection we have yet to experience takes my breath away, and in this moment, I want nothing more in the world than to connect with my soulmate, my friend, and the love of my life. Finally.

"Maggie," West whispers, his breath tickling my ear.

"Yes," I whisper back. Because I know him well enough to know what he wants without having to ask for it... and I know because I want it too. He takes my hand and leads me to his bedroom, sitting down on his bed and wrapping his arms securely around my lower back. I lean down and kiss him again, and he lifts my T-shirt off my body. I can't decide if I want to close my eyes and allow myself to give in completely to this moment or take him in, because the look in his stare as he runs his hands over my body is no-nonsense, like he has uncovered treasure that he has spent his life searching for and he can't look away. I know how he feels because I feel it too. He unclips my bra, and it surrenders to the floor. He continues to run his hands over me, exploring every inch with his touch and his kiss.

"West," I moan, thankful that finally, I don't have to worry about calling out the wrong name—and it feels fantastic. "West," I say again because I can.

West removes the remainder of my clothes and shimmies out of his. "Are you okay?" he asks, kissing my cheek.

"Of course," I answer between breaths. "Why wouldn't I be?"

"Because." He chuckles. "You're trembling."

"Oh," I reply as we climb under his covers. "I'm okay. I've actually never been better." And that is the truth, and I kiss him again, because if my words can't communicate to him how I am feeling, surely, my kiss will. And it must be a good one, because he pulls me on top of him in one quick, effort-less sweep, straddling my legs around him. He removes my hair tie, allowing my hair to surround his face. I collapse onto him, his hands tracing my back and up through my hair and down again. Every touch and every movement is better than I imagined in all the years I fantasized about this moment in my mind.

"I love you," he whispers as he pulls me closer.

My body surrounds his in every way possible, but I still want more. "I love you too," I moan between kisses. And after all the years of being Maggie Thatcher, the girl who just couldn't get it right, I close my eyes and release the part of me that haunts my soul with lies. The part of my being that so deceitfully convinces me that I'm not good enough. I free myself from the ideas and notions that once flew through my mind at the speed of light, and I open my heart in a way I never have before—I am free. I open my eyes again and stare into the soul of a man I have loved... *forever.* I can't hold him close enough, and I join with him in ways I never knew to be possible, and I understand in this moment, I have *finally* found my way. West.

CHAPTER TWENTY-TWO- NOW

MAGGIE

44 HOURS BEFORE THE BIG DAY

*W*aking up in the arms of West Young is something I have dreamed of for years, and now that it is happening, it is better than I could have ever imagined. I had grown to know him in many ways, but sleeping beside him had not been one of them. I study his dark hair and his perfect smile, and I wish for a moment that we could lie here forever. But unfortunately, my returning flight to Boston is departing from Phoenix at 2:00 p.m.

"West," I whisper. "West, we fell asleep."

West opens his eyes and smiles. "I was worried for a second that this whole thing was a dream," he confesses.

"You and me both."

"Want to get some lunch?" he asks, looking at his clock.

"I would, but I need to be at the airport in an hour."

His eyes open wide. "An hour? But you just got here."

"I know," I admit. "But honestly, I thought I was coming here to say the things I said to a man who is getting married. I really didn't think I needed more than ten minutes."

He nudges me playfully and kisses my forehead. "I know. I just don't want you to leave."

"There is just so much going on at work," I explain. "Art, your grandpa, has recently been reunited with a girl named Katie Roy, and he is a complete disaster."

West laughs at this and smiles. "Grandpa and Katie, eh? That would be something."

"It's a big deal. I think I should be there to help him."

"Didn't you take time off for my wedding?" he asks playfully.

"Yes. But that was before I knew it was a *fake* wedding. By the way, what exactly were you going to do when I showed up here for your wedding tomorrow?"

"I would have figured it out... probably give you the speech you gave me this morning." He laughs.

"Well, I'm glad I could do your dirty work for you. But I really should get back."

"Work will survive without you," he whispers, kissing me again and running his hands over my naked body.

"Uh-huh," I agree. "I suppose they will." I moan, pulling him on top of me once more as he kisses my ear, causing me to squirm and giggle from under him.

"Found the spot," he snickers, his breath heavy.

I nod, close my eyes, and throw my head back in defeat. "Yes," I gasp. "Yes, you did."

PART FOUR

CHAPTER TWENTY-THREE- NOW

MAGGIE

THE BIG DAY

*M*y Jimmy Choos click-clack against the pavement like they do on most days, but this time, things are different. Because for the first time in my entire life, I feel complete. It doesn't matter what happens to me today or what is on the other side of that door; I know who I am, and I know where I am going. And tonight, I will be in the arms of my totally hot boyfriend, whose plane lands in less than four hours and has promised to stay with me for the remainder of the summer.

"Good morning, Miss Thatcher," Seth greets per usual.

"Good morning, Seth," I reply. "I hope you have a good day today," I say, nudging him playfully in the arm.

"What's gotten into you?" he asks, and I can't tell if he's busting my chops or *really* asking.

"Nothing," I say. "I guess I'm just… happy."

"Maggie Thatcher is happy? Alert the media!"

"Have a good day, Seth."

* * *

AROUND NOON, Kendra calls me for my lunch order. I realize that I am caught up on my emails, so I take a trip up to the second floor to visit with Art, something I haven't done since I departed for my trip. I approach his room and knock on the door, but there is no answer.

"Art?" I call. "Art, are you in there?"

"You won't find him in there," a nurse says off-handedly as she passes by.

"Well then, where will I find him?"

She points down the hallway at Katie's room. My jaw drops, and my eyes grow wide. "Is he in there with her?"

She shrugs as if to say, *I don't know.*

"Wow... I... okay then. I guess I will see you around!"

I make my way back to my office as my phone starts vibrating in the pocket of my dress pants. It's Kendra calling again, and I am caught off guard. If I already ordered my lunch and Art Young is shacking up with Katie, then why does Kendra need me?

"Hi, Kendra," I say into my cell.

"You're not going to believe it," she groans.

"What? I just went to check on him!" I begin swapping my Jimmy Choos for my flip-flops.

"He's on the beach again," Kendra says with a sigh. "You might need your swimsuit for this one."

I fly down the stairs, simultaneously allowing my hand to slide down the metal banister. When I reach the beach, I shield my eyes from the sun with my hand and scan the water for Art Young, but what I see before me shocks me in a way I never imagined possible. Standing there, on the beach, is a line of residents and nursing home patients, some standing, some in wheelchairs, in front of the ocean... all smiling at me in a mischievous sort of way. "What is going on?" I ask under my breath. There, standing congregated before me, is a combination of residents and patients that I have grown to love over the years—Gwendoline Ellis, Joey Chase, Arthur Young, and many more. "What are you all doing out here?" I laugh a nervous laugh because deep in my soul, I know that something big is going down.

They all stare at me in an eerie sort of way until upbeat music begins to play from a portable Bluetooth speaker, and they all begin moving their bodies (as best they can) to the beat. One after another, they hold up handmade signs, most likely painted with supplies from the art center.

Gwendoline is the first to hold up her sign, and it reads, *Will.* I smile, wondering what these guys could possibly be up to. Joey Chase is the second to hold up a sign that reads, *You.* I know where this is going, and my heart starts to flutter. My knees grow weak as I realize this display of affection is one hundred percent the work of West. Arthur Young holds up a sign that reads, *Marry,* and then my dog Finley races from inside WVC with a sign attached to his collar that reads, *Me?*

"What on Earth?" I shout at the top of my lungs. "Finley? Hi, buddy!" I coo in my best dog-mom voice. I bend down, and he floods my face with kisses. "Finley, what are you doing here, boy?" Then my line of special residents applauds as West appears on the beach dressed in a navy-blue suit, looking more handsome than ever.

"West!" I cry. I can't help it, because though it has only been hours since I left him at the airport in Phoenix, it has felt like ages. "West! You're really here?"

He scoops me up and spins me around, dropping down to one knee before I have a chance to process what is really happening. He looks up at me, wide-eyed, holding a small velvet box. The music stops, and the residents and my coworkers gather around.

"Maggie," West starts. "Did you know that there are 7.7 billion people in this world? And with that, it means you have a 1-in-7.7 billion chance of meeting your best friend, let alone meeting your soulmate?"

I throw my hands to my face and squeal, unable to process what is happing. My knees grow weak again, and I need to hold on to his shoulder for support. "I…I do know that." Because for years, I have obsessed over the "never in a billion" promise.

"So that means not only have you overcome the odds and met your best friend, Maggie Thatcher, you have *defied* all odds and found your soulmate. And even still, as if you aren't a big enough overachiever, in one person—me—you have found your best friend, soulmate, and *future husband*." West opens the velvet box, revealing the most beautiful diamond engagement ring I have ever laid eyes on.

"West? Are you kidding me right now?"

"No, Maggie, I'm not kidding you. I've loved you from the first moment I laid eyes on you, and I have loved you more each day since. I'm sorry for all the years of confusion I put you through. I hope you can forgive me and make me the happiest man alive and marry me."

An unexpected tear runs down the side of my face, and West wipes it away; I am at a loss for words. I stare at the faces of the loved ones around me and take it all in. "Of course, West. Yes! Of course I will marry you!" The crowd cheers, and he spins me around. I bury my face in his neck and whisper, "Thank you," as he slides the ring onto my finger, and it fits perfectly.

Finley barks, and West bends down to pat him. "You are my one in a billion, Maggie Thatcher," he says, looking up at me. "I can't wait to spend the rest of my life with you."

He stands up, and we kiss as the crowd cheers again. Happiness washes over me, and I glance over West's shoulder to see my father smiling, clapping, and waving with the rest of my coworkers, patients, and friends.

"Wait!" Arthur's voice calls out from the crowd.

"Oh no," I gasp. "He is going to try and go for a swim again."

"What is it, Grandpa?"

"I have something to say," Art declares. "Many years ago, back in 1959, I fell in love. Not just puppy love or the kind of love one might see in the movies but real, true love, like the kind West and Maggie have demonstrated before us today."

"That's great, Grandpa—" West starts.

"I'm not done," Art snaps. "I loved Katie Roy more than I ever knew it was possible to love someone. And we were forbidden to be together by her father, Norman Roy. My heart was broken... so much so that even in my old age, I've been sulking around this facility and moping about a love I lost over sixty years ago... and wouldn't you know it? Just a couple of weeks ago, she walked right onto my doorstep!"

"Where is this going?" I whisper to West.

"No idea."

"So, this morning," Art continues, "I walked my old butt over to the nursing home here at WVC, and I had a conversation with her father. I explained to him that his daughter is my soulmate, and that even though over sixty years have gone by, I deserve the opportunity to be with her... and you know what? He *finally* gave me his blessing."

"I thought Norman Roy was nonverbal," I mutter under my breath.

West shrugs and claps his hands with everyone else as Art takes Katie by the hand. Her silver hair glistens in the sunlight, her smile beaming from ear to ear.

"So tell me, Katie, now that I have your father's blessing, will you do this old man a favor and marry me?"

"Yes, Arthur," Katie cries. "I will marry you."

The crowd cheers, and Art dips Katie back in a long and passionate kiss.

"Art is stealing your spotlight," I joke.

"I'll take it." He chuckles and kisses me again.

"I love you, West."

"I love you too. Thank you for coming out to Arizona and finding me," he says between kisses.

"Thank you for helping me find myself."

I close my eyes, lean in, and kiss Westly Arthur Young in the deepest, most passionate kiss of our lives. And as the residents and patients who have become my family over the years surround us with love and best wishes, I close my eyes and thank my lucky stars—billions of them—for West, my best friend, my soulmate, and my one true love.

CHAPTER TWENTY-FOUR-NOW

MAGGIE

TWO DAYS AFTER THE BIG DAY

I spin around in my office chair, fiddling with my engagement ring. It has been days since West's proposal, and I am still on cloud nine. He's been staying with me at the Seaberry, working from the cottage on "the Zoom," as Art likes to call it. And now as I watch the clock count down the minutes until I can leave, I believe I might just be the happiest woman in the world.

I scroll through my text messages, eager to pass the time.

Jordan: *Have you set a date yet?*

Maggie: *Not yet. You will be the first to know when it is set. After all, I need a maid of honor, right?*

Jordan: *OMG Maggie, I thought you would never ask.*

Maggie: *And Hayden will make a fantastic flower girl.*

My phone rings, and I am shocked to see my father's name flash across the screen. I answer. "Dad. Is everything okay?"

"Hi, sweetheart, yes, everything is fine. Can you meet me in my office in twenty minutes?"

"Uh, yes, sure," I respond, unsure as to what this might be regarding. I hang up the phone and call West on his cell.

"Hey, Mags," he says after the second ring. "What's up?"

"My dad wants to meet with me. I'm going to be a little late."

"No worries. Finley and I are here whenever you get home."

"Okay." I giggle. "Tell him I miss him."

"Oh, guess what? The house we looked at yesterday—they are still accepting offers."

"Really?" I shriek. "The one in York Harbor?"

"The one in York Harbor," he confirms. "Do you really love it?"

"I *really* love it. But, West… are you sure you are okay moving out this way?"

"I'm positive, Maggie. Like I said, I wasn't completely committed to the firm back in Scottsdale; I will find a place to practice law out this way."

I think for a moment. "Gwendoline Ellis has a grand-daughter, Cassidy Quinn. She recently opened an office in downtown York. I wonder if she is looking for a partner?"

"I'll check it out, for sure. See you when you get home. Love you, Maggie."

"Love you too," I say, smiling. I end the call and exit my office, making my way down the hallway to the elevator. I prepare to hit the button for the third floor, thinking I will go directly to my father's office, but I realize I never paid Kendra for lunch. I fish through the pocket of my dress pants and recover a ten-dollar bill and decide that I have time to run it over prior to my meeting with my dad. I take the elevator to the conference room and fling open the door to Kendra's office… and scream. Because Kendra Ferguson is sprawled out on her back on the conference room table; half-naked and standing over her with his pants down to his ankles and his ass exposed is Seth Jenson.

"Holy—oh my—" I cover my eyes with my hand, trying

desperately to unsee what I just walked in on. "I have money for lunch!" I call out, dropping the money on the desk and then dashing out of there as fast as my legs will carry me.

* * *

MOMENTS LATER, I am seated across from my father, still physically and emotionally in shock over Seth and Kendra. I gather my hair over my shoulder and shake my head, trying eagerly to get the image out of my mind. My father is perched at his mahogany desk, wearing his best suit, peering down at me from behind his designer glasses.

"You wanted to see me?" I asked, glancing at the time on my cell phone. The idea of West waiting for me at the Seaberry is at the forefront of my mind. Plus, I can't wait to tell him that I walked in on Seth and Kendra.

"Yes, Maggie. I did want to see you."

"Hopefully it's nothing bad?" I laugh nervously.

He tilts his glasses to the tip of his nose and smiles. "No, nothing bad. Maggie, it's good... You see, an administrative position has opened up here at WVC."

I drop my shoulders back and sit up straight in my chair. "Really?"

"Really. It is an administrative position that focuses solely on advocating for residents and their needs in all departments—independent, assisted, and nursing."

"No way."

"Way." He chuckles.

"So it would be an admin position, but I would still work with the residents."

"Yes," he affirms. "Let me ask you something, Maggie. When you think of the people here at WVC, what do you see?"

I think for a moment. "I see a community of people who

care for each other. A group of people who love the beach and the ocean, who want to have their freedoms but also the support of their friends and staff," I say confidently. "They want to be happy, but they understand that they just can't do it themselves anymore."

"And if you could change anything about it?"

"Change anything?"

"Yes, what would you change for them?"

I choose my words carefully. "One of the best things about WVC is that residents have the opportunity to live independently and then obtain support when they need it. But the thing is, we have them clumped into three very specific categories, and I just don't think all of them fit into one of the three molds."

My father nods and bites down on his pen. "Tell me more."

"Art Young, for example. He is ready for assisted living because he needs help with basic needs, but when it comes to outside time, he really doesn't *need* supervision. And then there are nursing home patients, like Gwendoline Ellis," I explain. "Just because she is a nursing home patient doesn't mean she should be stuck inside all day... the woman writes a blog, for heaven's sake. I'm sure if you ask her, she will tell you she feels cooped up when she is inside, and it's just not right."

He nods his head and smirks. "Thank you."

I study him for a moment, confusion flooding over me like ocean waves. "So, when can I interview?"

"You just did."

"Huh?"

"Welcome to the administrative team, Maggie. The patients here are lucky to have you."

I squeal with delight and throw my arms around my

father's shoulders. "Really? Are there other candidates, though? You know how I feel about playing the dad card."

"No other candidates… we actually designed this position *for* you. And you are the best woman for the job. I'm proud of you, Maggie. Your mother and I, we both are."

I hug my father and thank him again before bolting out of his office, eager to share my news with West. I grab my purse and fly down the hallway to the front door, where Seth stands, clothes disheveled, already holding the door open for me.

"Have a good evening, Miss Thatcher."

I shake my head and try to get the image of his naked buttocks out of my mind as he peers down at me, smiling. "Have a good evening, Seth," I say, pushing past him.

"You look great today, Miss Thatcher!"

I roll my eyes and glare up at him. "So, how long has that been going on?"

He raises his eyebrows in confusion. "How long has what been going on?"

I open my eyes wider, reach into my bag, and retrieve my berry lipstick. I apply it quickly, not letting him off the hook with my stare. "You and Kendra Ferguson."

"Me and Kendra?" he asks innocently.

"You and Kendra."

"Long enough." He sighs. "Long enough. But I mean it when I say it—I really do care about you."

"Uh-huh," I reply, tossing my lipstick back in my bag and pushing past him.

"Have a great night, Miss Thatcher!"

I stop, turn, and stare at him for a beat. "Hey, Seth?"

"Yeah?"

"Your fly is down."

EPILOGUE

*T*here was a time in my life when I couldn't face my reflection in the mirror. A time when words of encouragement, no matter how full of praise, just were not enough. When we build our lives on a foundation of how others view us, it is nearly impossible to have a successful future.

There was a time in my life when I made the wrong choice. And even though in the long run, it turned out to benefit me in ways I can't explain, it was still the wrong one at the time. I was surrounded by shame and regret, and no matter how hard I tried, I couldn't fill the emptiness in my soul.

There was a time in my life when I learned to forgive, and others forgave me. And because of this forgiveness, sacrifice, and unconditional love, we are all able to live happily ever after, in a sense. It is critical to remember, dear readers, that we are all human. And we are destined to make mistakes... and hopefully grow from them.

What I want to leave you with today, my dear friends, is no matter where you are in life, from age twenty to age one hundred, consider this: never forget where you came from, and always remember where you are going. Love yourself and love one another, *because in the end, all we truly have is each other. Never give up hope.*

ABOUT THE AUTHOR

Stacy Lee is the author of the Nubble Light Series. Stacy is a lifelong resident of New England. She lives in New Hampshire with her incredibly supportive husband, two beautiful children, and two well loved (spoiled) rescue pups. She enjoys spending time in the beautiful and historic town of York Beach, Maine with her family. The Nubble Lighthouse holds a special place in her heart.

Before she started writing women's fiction, Stacy received her bachelor's degree in elementary education with a teacher certification in grades K-8. She taught elementary school and writing courses to students for fourteen years while completing a graduate degree in elementary administration where she graduated with honors. After that, (in an effort to drive her husband completely crazy) decided to switch careers and go to Bible College, where she graduated with a Master's in Christian Ministry with a focus in Homiletics. Finally, when she got tired of taking college courses she decided to pursue her dream as an author. She is thankful for her husband and his ability to bring out the best in her...always.

TEN PERCENT OF MY HEART- BY STACY LEE

BOOK FOUR OF THE NUBBLE LIGHT SERIES

What do you do when you have nothing left to give?

As a twenty-three-year-old college graduate, Tessa Walker had it all. Psychology degree—check. School counseling position at the local elementary school—check. Everything was falling into place. Tessa was making significant strides with students, especially with a first grader named Beckett (Bex) who struggled with social anxiety. She adored her job and, for the first time, was able to rent her own apartment. She was even slightly convinced that maybe, just maybe, a proposal from her college sweetheart was right around the corner.

Then … it happened. A phone call from the local attorney in the middle of her twenty-two-minute lunch break. Bex's mother and father were tragically killed in a plane crash. There was a will, and for a reason unbeknownst to anyone involved, she was nominated as guardian for Bex. Court was scheduled for the following week. If willing, she would be appointed his guardian.

Now, as a successful career woman in her thirties

and single mom, Tessa's number one priority is her twelve-year-old adopted son. Gone are the days of romance, parties, and freedom. Tessa commits one hundred percent of herself to her career and her son ... until Bex writes a personal essay about how much he misses his *real* parents, and her heart all but shatters.

Tessa decides that it is time to spend the summer with Bex in York Beach, Maine, where his birth parents were born and raised. What starts as an intervention for her son's grief, turns into something much more, when she meets countless individuals who turn her life upside-down and refuse to let her settle for less. Tessa is convinced that she has nothing left to give, but someone special she is about to meet believes she is worthy of much more.

Made in the USA
Middletown, DE
06 February 2025

70195762R00104